Terry Pratchett was born in 194... as a journalist one day in 1965 an... work experience *meaning* something in those days. ... ... about every job it's possible to do in provincial journalism, except of course covering Saturday afternoon football, he joined the Central Electricity Generating Board and became press officer for four nuclear power stations. He'd write a book about his experiences if he thought anyone would believe it.

All this came to an end in 1987 when it became obvious that the Discworld series was much more enjoyable than real work. Since then the books have reached double figures and have a regular place in the bestseller lists. He also writes books for younger readers. Occasionally he gets accused of literature.

Terry Pratchett lives in Wiltshire with his wife Lyn and daughter Rhianna. He says writing is the most fun anyone can have by themselves.

Stephen Briggs was born in Oxford in 1951 and he still lives there, with his wife Ginny and their sons, Philip and Christopher.

In what would generally pass for real life he works for a small government department dealing with the food industry. However, as an escape to a greater reality, he has been involved for many years in the Machiavellian world of amateur dramatics, which is how he came to discover the Discworld.

Stephen is, by nature, a Luddite, but the Discworld has drawn him into the world of PCs, wordprocessing and electronic mail; he has even been known to paddle on the Internet. His other interests include sketching, back-garden ornithology and Christmas. He has never read *Lord of the Rings* all the way through.

Books by Terry Pratchett
THE COLOUR OF MAGIC*
THE LIGHT FANTASTIC*
EQUAL RITES*
MORT*
SOURCERY*
WYRD SISTERS*
PYRAMIDS*
GUARDS! GUARDS!*
ERIC (co-published with Gollancz)
MOVING PICTURES*
REAPER MAN*
WITCHES ABROAD*
SMALL GODS*
LORDS AND LADIES*
MEN AT ARMS*
SOUL MUSIC*
INTERESTING TIMES*
MASKERADE*
FEET OF CLAY

THE COLOUR OF MAGIC – GRAPHIC NOVEL
THE LIGHT FANTASTIC – GRAPHIC NOVEL
THE STREETS OF ANKH-MORPORK
(with Stephen Briggs)
THE DISCWORLD MAPP (with Stephen Briggs)
MORT – THE PLAY (adapted by Stephen Briggs)
WYRD SISTERS – THE PLAY
(adapted by Stephen Briggs)

MEN AT ARMS – THE PLAY
(adapted by Stephen Briggs)

GOOD OMENS (with Neil Gaiman)
STRATA
THE DARK SIDE OF THE SUN

TRUCKERS*
DIGGERS*
WINGS*
THE CARPET PEOPLE
ONLY YOU CAN SAVE MANKIND*
JOHNNY AND THE DEAD*
JOHNNY AND THE BOMB*

*also available in audio

and published by Corgi

HOG FATHER
THE UNADULTERATED CAT
(with Gray Jolliffe)
THE DISCWORLD COMPANION
(with Stephen Briggs)
TERRY PRATCHETT'S DISCWORLD QUIZBOOK
by David Langford

published by Gollancz

TERRY PRATCHETT'S
GUARDS! GUARDS!
the play

adapted for the stage by
STEPHEN BRIGGS

CORGI BOOKS

GUARDS! GUARDS! – THE PLAY
A CORGI BOOK : 0 552 14431 2

First publication in Great Britain

PRINTING HISTORY
Corgi edition published 1997

Guards! Guards! originally published in Great Britain by
Victor Gollancz Ltd
Copyright © Terry and Lyn Pratchett 1989

Stage adaptation copyright
© by Terry Pratchett and Stephen Briggs 1997

Discworld® is a registered trademark

Set in 12pt Monotype Ehrhardt by
Phoenix Typesetting, Ilkley, West Yorkshire.

Corgi Books are published by Transworld Publishers Ltd,
61–63 Uxbridge Road, London W5 5SA,
in Australia by Transworld Publishers (Australia) Pty Ltd,
15–25 Helles Avenue, Moorebank, NSW 2170
and in New Zealand by Transworld Publishers (NZ) Ltd,
3 William Pickering Drive, Albany, Auckland.

Reproduced, printed and bound in Great Britain by
Cox & Wyman Ltd, Reading, Berks.

INTRODUCTION

By the time we staged *Guards! Guards!* in 1993, we knew that the Discworld plays were a winner.

As with all the adaptations, there were difficult choices about which scenes should be sacrificed to try and keep the play down to a reasonable running time. We had also realised that Abingdon's medieval Unicorn Theatre was a part of the package; it has its shortcomings, but its ambience contributes much to the success of the shows.

Guards! Guards! had appealed to me for dramatisation since I first read it, but two things counted against it. First, it needed at least one swamp dragon, one orang-utan and one 60-foot dragon (the Unicorn's auditorium couldn't even *house* a 60-foot dragon!); second, it had only one female rôle, Lady Ramkin (we added a second – the Footnote – of whom more later).

Although, in adapting the book, I had in mind a number of compromises to allow some parts to be played by females, fortuitously, on this one occasion, we had very few available for the show and we proceeded with a clear conscience. Having overcome *that* obstacle, the dragons paled into insignificance!

This dramatisation was written with the Unicorn Theatre's restrictions, and the number of players I expected to have available, in mind. Really complicated scenic effects were virtually impossible. Anyone thinking of staging a Discworld play can be as imaginative as they like – call upon the might of Industrial Light & Magic, if it's within their budget. But *Guards! Guards! can* be staged with only a relatively modest outlay on special effects and the notes that accompany the text are intended to be a guide for those, like us, with limited budgets. Bigger groups, with teams of experts on hand, can let their imaginations run wild!

The script as it appears here is now tried and tested, but it isn't the *only* way to adapt the book. Other groups might make different choices. Some might have many more people available than we did, and they might want to add in 'crowd' scenes. What is important, though, is to ensure that a scene left in at one point in the play doesn't rely for part of its humour or logic on a scene you've cut elsewhere – or that a scene you've added as a show-stopper doesn't end up just slowing it down instead!

In short, though, our experience and that of other groups is that it pays to work hard on getting the costumes and lighting right, and to keep the scenery to little more than, perhaps, a few changes of level. One group with some resourceful technophiles achieved magnificent 'scenery' simply with sound effects and lighting ('dripping water' and rippling green light for a dungeon scene, for example). There's room for all sorts of ideas here. The Discworld, as it says in the book, is your mollusc.

Characterisation

Within the constraints of what is known and vital about each character, there is still room for flexibility of interpretation. With the main rôles, though, you have to recognise that your audiences will expect them to look as much like the book descriptions as possible. However, most drama clubs don't have a vast range from which to choose and it's the acting that's more important than the look of the player when it comes down to it!

The Footnote

When we staged *Mort*, we'd employed the device of allowing characters to step out of the play to comment on/ advance the action and, in some cases, to help to cover for scene changes. By the time I came to adapt *Guards! Guards!* the idea of using Terry's own literary device – the footnote – had been placed in my mind. This allowed us to include some good gags that would have been difficult to work into a character's dialogue and also, on occasion, to introduce a character to the audience.

Our Footnote was female. She wore tights, shoes decorated with spangly asterisks and a long white t-shirt bearing the legend –

*footnote

She carried a long black pole surmounted by a disc with an asterisk painted on it. Attached to the pole was a klaxon. Whenever the Footnote needed to make an announcement, she would sound the klaxon; the action on stage would freeze and she would then walk in, say her piece, re-sound the klaxon to re-start the action and depart. It worked well, and we employed the same device the following year in *Men at Arms*.

Death

On the Discworld he is a seven-foot tall skeleton of polished bone, in whose eye sockets there are tiny points of light (usually blue). He normally wears a robe –

apparently woven of absolute darkness – and sometimes also a riding cloak fastened with a silver brooch. He smells, not unpleasantly, of the air in old, forgotten rooms.

His scythe looks normal enough, except for the blade: it is so thin you can see through it, a pale blue shimmer that could slice flame and chop sound. The sword has the same ice-blue, shadow-thin blade, of the extreme thinness necessary to separate body from soul.

Having staged *Mort* a couple of years previously, we were fortunate in having 'invested' in a Death costume which was then available to do guest appearances in later shows. We had had Death's head-mask and gloves, robes and weapons made for us to our design by a firm called Creative Madness (now run as Spyder's FX, 2D Veale Close, Hatherlea, Okehampton, Devon). His eyes glowed blue, and the clear perspex blades of his sword and scythe – 'sharp' enough to see through!

Vimes
Captain of the Ankh-Morpork City Watch. Badge No. 177. An upright and honest man whose appointment to the Night Watch – regarded by all sensible people as a completely useless appendage to the running of the city – may have been the cause of his drinking problem. But it has also been suggested that he is in fact naturally more sober than other people. A state of acute sobriety is not one in which a man would like to view the society of Ankh-Morpork and he naturally sought to ameliorate this with a drink or five, and got the number wrong.

It is known that he was born in the Shades and would have joined the Watch shortly after leaving school if he had ever gone to school. Vimes never got the hang of ambition and worked his way sideways rather than up, and his promotion to Captain was simply the result of the sheer unthinkability of promoting any other watchman.

By his own account, he is a skinny, unshaven collection of bad habits marinated in alcohol. He is morose, cynical and ridiculously – and to his own embarrassment – soft-hearted in certain circumstances. He is almost certainly one of Nature's policemen; it has been said of him that his soul burns to arrest the Creator of the universe for getting it wrong.

He loathes kings, and hates undead and Assassins. He is also unashamedly speciesist – he deeply dislikes trolls and dwarfs, but in an almost proprietorial way, so that he has risked his life and badge to defend them merely so that he can continue to dislike them. He hates the city in the same way; it's his to hate.

Carrot

(Carrot Ironfoundersson). A dwarf (by adoption). His adoptive dwarf parents found him in the woods as a toddler, wandering near the bodies of his real parents, who had been victims of a bandit attack. Also in the wreckage of the cart was a sword, and a ring that was very similar to one recorded as having once been a part of the royal jewellery of Ankh.

He is six feet six inches tall with a big, honest forehead, mighty neck and impressively pink skin, due to scrubbing. He became known as Carrot not because of his red hair, kept short for reasons of hygiene, but because of his shape – the kind of tapering shape a boy gets through clean living, healthy eating and good mountain air in huge lungfuls. When Carrot flexes his muscles, other muscles have to move out of the way first. He has a punch which even trolls have learned to respect. He walks with a habitual stoop, which comes of being two metres tall but living with dwarfs. Like all dwarfs, when away from home he writes at least once a week.

His adoptive parents, embarrassed at his size and the fact that he had reached puberty at what, in dwarf terms, is about playgroup age, realised that he needed to be among his own kind. They arranged for him to join the Night Watch in Ankh-Morpork because, they had been told, it would make a man of him.

Being very literal-minded is a dwarfish trait. It is one which Carrot shares. In the whole of his life (prior to his arrival in Ankh-Morpork) no-one ever really lied to him or gave him an instruction that he wasn't meant to take literally. He is direct, honest, good-natured and honourable in all his dealings. He still thinks everyone is decent underneath and would get along just fine if only they made the effort. He is genuinely, almost supernaturally likeable. And he is astonishingly simple – which is not at all the same as 'stupid'. It is just that he sees the world shorn of all the little lies and prevarications that other people erect in order to sleep at night.

After a few initial setbacks, Carrot has had an exemplary career as a policeman, often helped by the fact that people confuse his simplicity with idiocy.

He has a crown-shaped birthmark at the top of his left arm. Coupled with his sword, his charisma, his natural leadership, and his deep and almost embarrassing love of Ankh-Morpork, this rather suggests that he is the long-lost rightful heir to the throne of the city.

He seriously believes that to be a policeman is to be the guardian of civilisation. He is, in fact, very happy in his job.

Colon

Sergeant in the Ankh-Morpork City Watch. Age believed to be about sixty. A fat man with a huge, red face like a harvest moon. He is married with three grown-up children, and some grand-children. He likes the peace and quiet of the night; he owes thirty years of happy marriage to the fact that Mrs Colon works all day gutting fish and he works all night.

Fred Colon used to be in an army (city unknown) but has been in the City Watch for thirty years, and he has known Captain Vimes for over twenty years. He smokes a pipe, and wears sandals with his Watch uniform, along with a breastplate with impressive pectoral muscles embossed on it, which his chest and stomach fit into in the same way that jelly fits into a mould.

He is the sort of man who, in a military career, will automatically gravitate to the post of sergeant. As a civilian, his natural rôle would be something like a sausage butcher – some job where a big, red face and a tendency to sweat even in frosty weather are practically part of the specification.

Nobby

Corporal C.W.St J. (Cecil Wormsborough St John). A corporal in the Ankh-Morpork Night Watch. A four-foot tall, pigeon-chested, bandy-legged man, with the muscle tone of an elastic band and a certain resemblance to a chimpanzee. The only reason you can't say that Nobby is close to the animal kingdom is that the animal kingdom would move further away. Nobby is actually smaller than many dwarfs (er . . . we compromised a bit on this!).

He is rumoured to have terrible personal habits, although these appear to be no more than a penchant for petty theft (usually from people too unconscious or, for preference, too dead to argue) an ability to do tricks with his facial boils, and a liking for folk dancing.

Men like Nobby can be found in any armed force. Although their grasp of the minutiae of the regulations is usually encyclopaedic, they take good care never to be promoted beyond, perhaps, corporal. He smokes incessantly, but the weird thing is that any cigarette smoked by Nobby becomes a dog-end almost instantly but remains a dog-end indefinitely or until lodged behind his ear, which is a sort of nicotine Elephants' Graveyard.

Nobby is known to have served as a quartermaster in the army of the Duke of Pseudopolis. There are rumours that he had to join the Watch after items missing from the stores were found in his kit. Since the items were the entirety of the store inventory, Nobby's kit at the time consisted of two warehouses.

Lord Vetinari

First name Havelock. Age uncertain. Background unavailable. Reputedly trained at the Assassins' Guild school. Now supreme ruler of the city of Ankh-Morpork, to which he is totally devoted. Tall, thin, and generally to be seen wearing black.

He appears to have survived by being equally distrusted and disliked by all interest groups in the city but also by carefully not being as unpopular as every interest group is to all the others.

Technically, Vetinari seems to have given in to every demand of every Guild for years, so the Guilds are driving themselves mad wondering why he is therefore still in charge. His genius lies in the realisation that everyone craves stability even more than they hunger after justice or truth. This policy is dimly perceived by the more intelligent Guild leaders in the city. Annoying as the Patrician is, however, it is so easy to think of someone worse.

He is entirely without vices in any normal sense of the word. If he had any, we can be sure some Guild or other would have made use of them by now. It is true that he has banned street theatre and hangs mime artists upside down in a scorpion pit opposite a sign which says 'Learn The Words', but this may be considered an excusable peccadillo or possibly an amusing character trait. He does have a small and very old terrier, called Wuffles, to which he is said to be quite attached.

Lord Vetinari lives in what was once the royal family's Winter Palace in Morpork. He manages the city either from a wooden seat at the foot of the steps on which is the ancient golden throne of the city, or more usually from the Oblong Office, high in the palace. This is where he gathers information. People tell him things, for all sorts of reasons. He has a bedroom. He presumably sleeps.

Lady Ramkin

Sybil Deirdre Olgivanna. The Ramkin Family Motto is: NON SUMET NULLUS PRO RESPONSO (Never Take No For An Answer).

Lady Ramkin is the richest woman in Ankh-Morpork.

She is a toweringly big lady, with a mass of chestnut hair (a wig – no-one who has much to do with dragons keeps their own hair for long). The Ramkins have never bred for beauty; they've bred for healthy solidity and big bones, and Lady Sybil is the shining result.

For almost all of her life she has apparently confined her own personal breeding to swamp dragons, which she keeps in pens behind the house, and she is the tower of strength behind the Sunshine Sanctuary for Sick Dragons. For dragon handling, she wears huge and fearsomely padded armour. She is the author of several self-published volumes on the diseases of the dragon, which is a fruitful and probably endless field of study.

Costumes

We played most of the characters around the Georgian period, although the City Watch were attired in uniforms of the English Civil War period, which helped to point up the anachronism that they are viewed as by their citizens, particularly when they are placed against the Patrician's guard, whom we costumed in eighteenth-century British army uniforms.

We were lucky enough to be able to borrow helmets, back- and breast-plates from the Sealed Knot for *Guards! Guards!*; one of the cast was an ex-member and the production timed neatly into a part of the year when the Knot were fairly inactive and members could spare us some stuff.

The Brethren all wore long, black, hooded robes with silver half-masks (gold for the Supreme Grand Master). When Brother Watchtower breaks his Brethren mask, we had him replace it with a fox mask, which looked very incongruous peering out of his black robe!

Our Patrician wore a long, voluminous black robe over a high necked 'Russian peasant' black shirt, black trousers and boots. On his head he wore a black skull cap. The effect was one of power combined with ecclesiastical austerity.

Scenery

Virtually none. We had city coats of arms decorating the set (Lady Ramkin's, the Watch and the City itself). Other than that, we used the minimum of furniture necessary to establish the settings (a multi-purpose table and chairs, a door with a sliding grille for the Brethren, a bed (easily stowable).

Special Effects
Other little bits and pieces included:

Errol
We had Errol made for us by Spyder's FX in Okehampton (01837 811033). In fact, we had two made. One was for carrying – a sort of Rod Hull's Emu, which emerged from a false arm in a specially-constructed dragon-handler's jacket. This one could be operated by the 'handler' so that his head could turn, his mouth open and close and his eyes could glow red. The other Errol was for flying and was constructed in a flying pose with wings outstretched, carefully-concealed hanging loops – oh, and a fireproof container in his, erm, well in his bottom to take a smoke pellet! This Errol we had concealed on stage throughout the play in a box with a trick lid. When the due moment came, our Errol took off, to the strains of the theme from *The Battle of Britain*, and moved vertically up the back of the stage to disappear into a masked area in the 'flies'.

The Librarian
We'd cruelly cut him out of *Mort* the previous year, so we felt we owed it to him to get Spyder's FX to make us a costume for *Guards! Guards!* He looked very good indeed, but we staged the play in the summer and the actor who played our Librarian found that being encased in rubber and fur fabric, under stage lighting, is not conducive to keeping cool.

xvii

We had ours made for us because we hadn't been able to track down an orang-utan costume for hire. You, dear reader, might like to know that the Orangutan Foundation do now have an orang-utan costume that they may be prepared to loan to a careful user – subject to its being returned in at least as good a condition as that in which it went out, and to a donation for their organisation. They can be contacted via Ashley Leiman, Orangutan Foundation, 7 Kent Terrace, London, NW1 4RP (Tel/Fax: 0171 724 2912).

The Dragon

Well, as you'll have gathered, the Unicorn Theatre in Abingdon (where *Guards! Guards!* was premièred) could not house a sixty-foot dragon. But – we argued – the best bits of films such as *Jaws* and *Alien* are those scenes where the monster is left to the audience's imagination (a glimpse of the shark's fin, a quick vision of the alien's slavering jaws); why couldn't we use the audience to build our dragon in their own minds?

So we used a variety of effects to place our dragon 'behind the audience' in the fourth wall of the stage. When the Dragon appeared, we had musicians strike up a threatening *Jaws*-type theme, and played a track of flapping leathery wings over the sound system. When it flamed, we flooded the stage with blood-red light, an actor performed the roar live into an off-stage mike, played through speakers behind the audience (as was the Dragon's speaking voice) and we jetted twin streams of smoke from a remotely operated smoke machine sited in the roof beams of our theatre. The combination of all these was surprisingly effective.

Other Effects

At the start of the play, we had a rain effect lamp playing on the stage which, when combined with an SFX tape of torrential rain, gave a nicely soggy feel to the opening scene outside the meeting room. We also made use of a flame effect lamp when Vimes and Sybil are watching the dragon flame the city. When Vimes first threatens the crowd with Errol, we used a theatrical flash pod for Vimes's first 'shot'. We also used smoke pellets, both for the dragon pens at Lady Ramkin's and for Errol's bottom for his flight scene.

Stephen Briggs
May 1997

TERRY PRATCHETT'S
GUARDS! GUARDS!

adapted for the stage by Stephen Briggs

CAST OF CHARACTERS

Carrot
Voice at Door
Brother Doorkeeper
Lupine Wonse/Grand Master
Footnote
Brother Plasterer
Zebbo Mooty
The Patrician
Corporal Nobbs
Sergeant Colon
C.M.O.T. Dibbler
Second Citizen
Bunting Carrier
First Guard
First Warrior
Archchancellor
First Worthy

Carrot's Dad
Brother Fingers
Captain Vimes
Knowlessman
Brother Watchtower
Brother Dunnykin
Death
Urdo Van Pew
The Librarian
Lady Sybil Ramkin
First Citizen
Dragon
Servant
Second Guard
Second Warrior
Chief Assassin
Second Worthy

Dwarfs, Citizens

Play first performed by the Studio Theatre Club
on 8 to 12 June 1993
at the Unicorn Theatre, Abingdon

SCENE 1 – THE PROLOGUE

The dwarf mines. Dark and gloomy. A number of vertically challenged people cross the stage, whistling, and carrying picks, lanterns, shovels, etc. At the end of the line is Carrot.

CARROT'S DAD (*off stage*)
Carrot! (*entering*) Ah, Carrot, lad. Erm, good.

CARROT
Hello, Dad. Mam said you wanted a word with me.

(They are now standing next to each other, Carrot's Dad on his knees – Toulouse-Lautrec style – Carrot a good six feet plus)

CARROT'S DAD
Er, yes. Erm. Well now, Carrot, er, I expect you've noticed that you are not like other dwarfs.

CARROT
How do you mean?

CARROT'S DAD
I . . . er, now look, lad, I don't want to make a big thing out of this. I mean, your mam and me thought you'd just grow out of it, see?

CARROT
Grow out of what?

CARROT'S DAD

Growing. But you didn't. So we thought you should spend more time with your own kind.

CARROT

But you're my own kind.

CARROT'S DAD

Nay, lad. I'm sorry to be short with you [*NOTE Yes, these are the jokes!*], but the fact is . . . you're human.

CARROT

What, like Mr Varneshi, you mean? (*Carrot's Dad nods*) But I can't be. You're a dwarf, Mam's a dwarf. I've GOT to be a dwarf.

CARROT'S DAD (*clearing throat*)

The thing is . . . we found you in the woods, see. When you was a baby. There'd been a robbery. You was lying in the verge next to a burned-out cart, see.

CARROT

So I'm not a dwarf, then?

CARROT'S DAD

Only by adoption. Sorry.

Anyway, I asked Mr Varneshi for his advice. You know, what sort of job we should get you, with humans an' that. He said that a career in the Ankh-Morpork City Watch would make a man of you.

CARROT

But—

4

CARROT'S DAD (*taking a letter out of his pocket*)
AND so I wrote to their headman (*peers at letter*) a Mr Lupine . . . Squiggle PP Patrician. You've been accepted!

CARROT
Wow! The Ankh-Morpork City Watch.

CARROT'S DAD
So you're to report to him pronto, if not sooner.

But before you go, there's this.

(*Magical chord and light. Carrot's Dad holds up sword.*)

We found it next to you in the wreckage of the cart. We took it along to Miss Garlick, the witch, to see if it was magical like . . .

(*Light and chords out*)

But she said no.

Quite the most unmagical sword she'd ever seen she said.

CARROT
Oh.

CARROT'S DAD
And there's these, too. Mr Varneshi asked me to give them to you. Belonged to his great-grandfather, he said, when he was in the City Watch.

(*He hands over a book*)

CARROT
The Laws and Ordinances of the Cities of Ankh and Morpork.

CARROT'S DAD
That's what the Watch has to know, he said. You have to know all the Laws to be a good officer.

CARROT
Then I shall learn them straight away.

CARROT'S DAD
And lastly there's this.

(*He hands him the Protective. Ours was a cricket box, adorned with metal paint, studs and so on*)

CARROT
What is it? Some sort of sling?

CARROT'S DAD
It's a . . . protective. Humans wear them in battle, like, to protect their, erm, vitals, as it were.

CARROT
It's a bit small, Dad.

CARROT'S DAD
That's because you don't wear it on your head, lad.

(*He pulls Carrot down to him and whispers in his ear. Carrot looks amazed.*)

Mr Varneshi swore his great granddad found it very

6

useful. 'If my great granddad hadn't worn that protective,' he told me, 'I wouldn't be here today.'

CARROT
What did he mean by that?

CARROT'S DAD
I, er, well, erm . . . never mind about that, lad. You've packing to do and so on. Off you go.

But promise me lad, that you won't forget your roots here. When you've made your fortune in the big city, promise me you'll never look down on me and your Mam.

CARROT
I promise.

(*He strides heroically off as the lights black out*)

SCENE 2 – A STREET IN ANKH-MORPORK.
NIGHT

It is raining heavily. Hissing down. Through the rain comes a robed figure (Brother Fingers), huddled against the weather, and carrying a book. He approaches a door and takes out of his pocket a small book which he refers to while he executes a 'complicated' knock: Page one – knock (check book again, turn page) Page two – knock, knock (check book again, turn page) Page three – knock, knock, knock, and so on up to about 'seven' when a grille in the door opens suddenly and a face peers through.

VOICE
  Yes?

BROTHER FINGERS
  The significant owl hoots in the night.

VOICE
  Yet many grey lords go sadly to the masterless men.

BROTHER FINGERS
  Hooray, Hooray for the spinster's sister's daughter.

VOICE
  To the axeman, all supplicants are the same height.

BROTHER FINGERS
  Yet verily, the rose is within the thorn.

8

VOICE
The good mother makes bean soup for the errant boy.

BROTHER FINGERS (*after a pause*)
What?

VOICE
The good mother makes bean soup for the errant boy.

BROTHER FINGERS (*after another pause*)
Are you sure the ill-built tower doesn't tremble mightily at a butterfly's passage?

VOICE
Nope. Bean soup it is. Sorry.

BROTHER FINGERS
What about the cagéd whale?

VOICE
What about it?

BROTHER FINGERS
It should know nothing of the mighty deeps, if you must know.

VOICE
Oh, the cagéd whale. You want the Elucidated Brethren of the Ebon Night. Three doors down.

BROTHER FINGERS
Who're you then?

VOICE
  We're the Illuminated and Ancient Brethren of Ee.

BROTHER FINGERS
  I thought you met over in Treacle Street.

VOICE
  Yeah, well, you know how it is. The fretwork club have
  the room Tuesdays. There was a bit of a mix-up.

BROTHER FINGERS
  Oh? Well, thanks anyway.

VOICE
  My pleasure.

  (*The grille slams shut. Brother Fingers makes his way
  over to the other door [or, in our case, made his way
  around the stage and back to the same door again]. He
  repeats the 'knock' business up to about 'three' when the
  grille opens and another face looks out*)

BROTHER DOORKEEPER
  Yes?

BROTHER FINGERS
  Look, The significant owl hoots in the night, all right?

BROTHER DOORKEEPER
  Yet many grey lords go sadly to the masterless men.

BROTHER FINGERS
  Hooray, Hooray for the spinster's sister's daughter, OK?

BROTHER DOORKEEPER
To the axeman, all supplicants are the same height.

BROTHER FINGERS
Yet verily, the rose is within the thorn. It's pissing down out here. You do know that, do you?

BROTHER DOORKEEPER
Yes.

BROTHER FINGERS (*after a sigh*)
The cagéd whale knows nothing of the mighty deeps. If it makes you any happier.

BROTHER DOORKEEPER
The ill–built tower trembles mightily at a butterfly's passage.

BROTHER FINGERS (*grabbing the grille*)
Now let us in. I'm soaked.

BROTHER DOORKEEPER
These deeps . . . did you say mighty or nightly?

BROTHER FINGERS
Mighty, I said. Mighty deeps. On account of being, you know, deep. It's me, Brother Fingers.

BROTHER DOORKEEPER
It sounded like nightly to me.

BROTHER FINGERS
Look, do you want the bloody book or not? I don't have to do this. I could be at home in my bed.

BROTHER DOORKEEPER
You sure it was mighty?

BROTHER FINGERS
Listen, I know how deep the bloody deeps are all right.
I knew how mighty they were when you were a perishing
neophyte. Now will you open this door?

BROTHER DOORKEEPER
Well . . . all right.

(*There is a noise of bolts being drawn back.*)

Would you mind giving it a push? The Door of
Knowledge Through Which the Untutored May Not
Pass sticks something wicked in the damp.

(*As Brother Fingers puts his shoulder to the door, the
lights change to the door of the Broken Drum, where
Vimes can be heard bellowing off stage. He bursts on,
having been apparently pushed from off stage.*)

VIMES
All right . . . well, you can stick your beer. I don't need
you, mate. (*loudly*) I'm Captain Vimes of the Night
Watch, I am. This is my city.

Bad day for the Watch. Lost old Gaskin. Poor old
Gaskin . . . Poor old Vimes. Went off after the funeral
and got drunk. No, not drunk. Another word, ending in
'er'. Drunker, that was it. Something else now. What was
it? Oh yes, night-time . . . time for duty. Not for Gaskin
though. Have to get a new chap. New chap coming
anyway. Got a letter. Some stick from the hicks . . .

Tick from the Shicks. Sod it. Ankh-Morpork's finest.

(*He passes the door to the Elucidated Brethren*)

Ah, Tuesday. The Elucidated Brethren of the Ebon thingy. Bloody secret societies. Up to no wossname . . . good, I bet.

(*As Vimes exits, the klaxon sounds and the Footnote enters*)

FOOTNOTE
They may be called the Palace Guard, the City Guard, or the Patrol. Whatever the name, their purpose in any work of heroic fantasy is identical: it is, around about Chapter Three, or ten minutes into the play, to rush into the room, attack the hero one at a time . . . and be slaughtered.

No-one ever asks them if they wanted to.

This play is dedicated to those fine men.

(*Klaxon. Black out*)

13

SCENE 3 – MEETING HALL OF THE ELUCIDATED BRETHREN. GLOOMY INTERIOR

Moody music (we used a bit from the 'Magic Flute' – secret society, geddit?) The Brethren – all in long, black, hooded robes and half-masks – process onto the stage, forming a circle open at the audience's side. Last to enter is the Supreme Grand Master (Lupine Wonse – although the audience shouldn't know it yet), centre stage.

LUPINE WONSE

I call the Unique and Supreme Lodge of the Elucidated Brethren to order. Is the Door of Knowledge sealed fast against heretics and knowlessmen, Brother Doorkeeper?

BROTHER DOORKEEPER

Stuck solid. It's the damp. I'll bring my plane in next week . . . soon have it . . .

LUPINE WONSE

All right, all right. Just a yes would have done. Art all here who art here? And be it well for a knowlessman that he should not be here, for he would be taken from this place and his gaskin slit, (*one of the Brethren tentatively puts up his hand*) his moules shown to the four winds, his welchet torn asunder with many hooks and his figgin placed on a spike yes what is it?

KNOWLESSMAN
Sorry, did you say Elucidated Brethren? Sorry, sorry, wrong Society, I'm afraid. Must have taken a wrong turning. I'll just be going then, if you'll excuse me . . .

(and he shuffles out)

LUPINE WONSE
And his figgin placed upon a spike. Are we quite finished? Any more knowlessmen happen to drop in on their way somewhere else? Right. Fine. So glad. Perhaps we can get on with it.

(Klaxon. Footnote enters. Action freezes)

FOOTNOTE
A figgin is described in the *Dictionary of Eye-Watering Words* as a 'small short-crust pastry containing raisins'. The dictionary would have been invaluable to the Supreme Grand Master when he thought up the Brotherhood's oaths, since it also includes welchet: 'a type of waistcoat worn by clock-makers', gaskin: 'a shy, grey-brown bird of the coot family' and moules: 'a game of skill and dexterity, involving tortoises'.

(Klaxon. Footnote exits, action continues)

LUPINE WONSE
Brethren, tonight we have matters of profound importance to discuss. The good governance, nay, the very future of our city, the great city of Ankh-Morpork, lies in our hands.

Do we not know that the city is in thrall to men who wax fat on their ill-gotten gains while better men are held back and forced into virtual servitude?

Yet it was not always thus. There was once a golden age, when those worthy of respect were justly rewarded. (*Brother Watchtower puts up his hand*) An age of chivalry, an age— yes, Brother Watchtower?

BROTHER WATCHTOWER
Are you talking about when we had kings?

LUPINE WONSE
Yes, very good, Brother Watchtower.

BROTHER WATCHTOWER
There aren't any more kings, is the point I'm making.

LUPINE WONSE
HOWEVER . . . it may not be the ancient line of Kings of Ankh-Morpork is as defunct as often imagined. My researches in the ancient scrolls reveal this.

   (*Brother Watchtower puts up his hand*)

Yes?

BROTHER WATCHTOWER
Are you saying there's some sort of heir to the throne hanging around somewhere?

LUPINE WONSE
That may be the case, yes.

16

BROTHER PLASTERER
Yeah, there used to be some old prophecy or something . . . 'Yea, the King will come, bringing Law and Justice . . .'

BROTHER WATCHTOWER
Nah, you can't trust old legends.

BROTHER DUNNYKIN
Why not?

BROTHER WATCHTOWER
Cos they're legendary, that's why.

BROTHER DOORKEEPER
Of course, in the old days it was easy.

BROTHER WATCHTOWER
Why?

BROTHER DOORKEEPER
He just had to kill a dragon.

LUPINE WONSE
Aah. What an interesting idea.

BROTHER WATCHTOWER
Wouldn't work. There's no big dragons these days.

LUPINE WONSE
But . . . there could be.

BROTHER WATCHTOWER

What, the real thing? Great big scales and wings? Breath like a blast furnace? Them big claw things on his feet?

LUPINE WONSE

Talons? Oh yes, as many as you want.

BROTHER WATCHTOWER

What do you mean, as many as I want?

LUPINE WONSE

I would hope it's self-explanatory, Brother Watchtower. If you want dragons, you can have dragons. YOU can bring a dragon here. Now. In the city.

BROTHER WATCHTOWER

Me?

LUPINE WONSE

All of you, I mean us. And it would obey your every command. (*pause*) You can control it. You can make it do whatever you want.

BROTHER PLASTERER

What? A real dragon?

LUPINE WONSE

Yes, a real one. Not a little pet swamp dragon. The genuine article.

BROTHER PLASTERER

But I thought they were, you know, miffs.

LUPINE WONSE

They were *myths* and they were real. When I was undergoing my tuition by the Secret Masters, among the many secrets from the Heart of Being was the current location of noble dragons. And they can be summoned from it. Did you manage to acquire that item from the magic library in the Wizards' University, Brother Fingers?

BROTHER FINGERS

Yes, Supreme Grand Master

(*He hands it over. At this stage, the audience still can't see that the back of the book is badly fire-damaged*)

LUPINE WONSE

Excellent. This book . . . gives specific instructions.

BROTHER PLASTERER

It's just in a book?

LUPINE WONSE

No ordinary book. This is the only copy. It's in the handwriting of Tubul de Malachite, a great student of dragon lore. He summoned dragons of all sizes. And so can you.

BROTHER WATCHTOWER

Um. (*pause*) Sounds a bit like, you know . . . magic to me. I mean, not wishing to question your supreme wisdomship and that, but . . . well . . . you know . . . magic . . .

BROTHER PLASTERER
Yeh.

BROTHER DUNNYKIN
Huh. Wizards. What do they know about a day's work.

BROTHER DOORKEEPER
It's only waving your arms and chanting, when all's said and done.

(*A general chorus of agreement.*)

LUPINE WONSE
Then we are agreed then, Brethren? You are prepared to practise magic?

BROTHER PLASTERER
Oh practise. I don't mind practising. So long as we don't have to do it for real.

LUPINE WONSE (*thumping the book*)
I mean carry out real spells! Put the city back on the right lines! Summon a dragon!!

BROTHER DOORKEEPER
And the, if we get this dragon, the rightful king'll turn up . . . just like that?

LUPINE WONSE
Yes.

BROTHER WATCHTOWER
Yeah. Stands to reason. 'Cos of destiny and so on.

BROTHER PLASTERER

We-ell. It won't get out of hand, will it?

LUPINE WONSE

I assure you, Brother Plasterer, that you can give it up any time you like. Now, Brethren, you have all brought the items as requested?

(*General murmuring*)

Place them in the Circle of Conjuration. What is this?

BROTHER DUNNYKIN

's a amulet. 's very powerful. Bought it off a man. Guaranteed. Protects you against crocodile bites.

LUPINE WONSE

Are you sure you can spare it?

(*A few titters*)

Less of that, brothers. Bring magical things, I said. Not cheap jewellery and rubbish. Good grief, this city is lousy with magic! What are these things, for heaven's sake?

BROTHER PLASTERER

They're stones.

LUPINE WONSE

I can see that. Why're they magical?

BROTHER PLASTERER

They've got holes in them, Supreme Grand Master. Everyone knows that stones with holes in them are magical.

LUPINE WONSE (*wearily*)

Right, fine, OK. If that's how we're going to do it, that's how we're going to do it. If we get a dragon six inches long we'll all know the reason why. Won't we, Brother Plasterer. Brother Plasterer? Sorry, I didn't hear what you said? Brother Plasterer?

BROTHER PLASTERER

I said yes, Supreme Grand Master.

LUPINE WONSE

Very well. So long as that's understood. And now, if we are all quite ready . . .

BROTHER WATCHTOWER

But you haven't told us what to do yet, Supreme Grand Master.

LUPINE WONSE

Well it's obvious. You have to focus your concentration. Think hard about dragons. All of you.

BROTHER DOORKEEPER

That's all, is it?

LUPINE WONSE

Yes.

BROTHER DOORKEEPER
Don't we have to chant a mystic prune or something?

(*Brother Dunnykin puts up his hand*)

LUPINE WONSE (*after a short pause*)
You can if you like. Now . . . I want you— YES WHAT IS IT BROTHER DUNNYKIN?

BROTHER DUNNYKIN
Don't know any mystic prunes, Supreme Grand Master. Not to what you might call chant . . .

LUPINE WONSE
HUM! Right (*opens book*) Here we go . . . (*reads aloud*) Wonsu Otem Ocnogard Elbir Rettubta Ergo!

(*Black out. Sound of leathery wings. Klaxon. Enter Footnote*)

FOOTNOTE
It was about to be the worst night of his life for Zebbo Mooty, thief third class, and it wouldn't have made him feel any better to have known that it was also going to be his last. The rain was keeping people indoors and he was way behind on his thieving quota.

(*We cross-fade to a street in Ankh-Morpork. Zebbo Mooty creeps on, dagger outstretched before him. He peers out towards the audience, he spies something . . .*)

ZEBBO MOOTY
Right, mate, give us your— ooh, shi—

23

(There is a terrible roar. The stage is swamped with light. All blacks out. Zebbo falls to the ground. As the lights come up again, he gets to his feet. Death is now on stage. Zebbo is confused and at first does not see Death)

DEATH
HELLO.

ZEBBO MOOTY
What was that?

DEATH
A DRAGON, I THINK.

ZEBBO MOOTY
'Ere, who're you?

DEATH
DON'T YOU KNOW?

ZEBBO MOOTY *(noticing the 'body' at his feet)*
Oh, I'm dead, then, am I?

DEATH
'FRAID SO.

ZEBBO MOOTY
I thought you didn't turn up for the likes of me.

DEATH
I TURN UP FOR EVERYONE.

ZEBBO MOOTY
No, no, I mean in person, like.

DEATH
SOMETIMES. ON SPECIAL OCCASIONS,
PERHAPS.

ZEBBO MOOTY
Right. Being killed by a dragon counts as a special
occasion, I suppose.

DEATH
YES.

ZEBBO MOOTY
'Ere, when I was a kid a fortune-teller told me I'd
die in me own bed, surrounded by grieving great-
grandchildren. What do you think of that?

DEATH (*after a moment's pause*)
I THINK SHE WAS WRONG.

(*Lights cross-fade back to the Brethren*)

LUPINE WONSE
We did it! The dragon! It came! I felt it!

BROTHER PLASTERER
We never saw nothing.

BROTHER WATCHTOWER
I might of seen something—

LUPINE WONSE
No, not here. You hardly want it to materialise here, do you? It was out there, in the city. Just for a few seconds . . . Look!

(*He picks up the box/bowl that had contained their magical items. It is full of ash*)

BROTHER FINGERS
Sucked dry. I'll be damned.

BROTHER DUNNYKIN
Three dollars that amulet cost me.

LUPINE WONSE
But it proves it works. Don't you see, you fools? It works! We CAN summon dragons!

BROTHER FINGERS
Could be a bit expensive in magical items.

BROTHER DUNNYKIN
Three dollars it was. No rubbish.

LUPINE WONSE
Power . . . does not come cheap.

BROTHER WATCHTOWER
Very true. Not cheap. Cor, we did it, though, dint we! We only went and did some bloody magic, right?

LUPINE WONSE
You have all done exceptionally well.

BROTHER DUNNYKIN
Should've been six dollars, but he said he'd cut his own throat and sell it for three dollars.

BROTHER FINGERS
Yeah, we got the hang of it, all right! Dint hurt a bit. And we dint get et by tooth fairies from out the woodwork neither, Brother Plasterer, I couldn't help noticing.

BROTHER PLASTERER
Hang on, though. Where's this dragon gone?

LUPINE WONSE
We summoned it. It came. But only so long as the magic lasted. Then it went back. If we want it to stay longer, we need more magic. Understand? And that is what we must get.

(*The Brothers start to leave, Brother Dunnykin still mumbling to himself. Lupine Wonse comes downstage to soliloquise.*)

LUPINE WONSE
Well, dear Tu . . .

BROTHER DUNNYKIN (*to himself, as he departs*)
That's three dollars I shan't see again in a hurry—

LUPINE WONSE
Shut up!! Well, dear Tubul de Malachite, I've done it. Easier than I expected, though, with this bunch of simpletons. Just as well they didn't see the state of the end of your book.

(He turns to the back; it is badly fire-damaged)

YOU were clearly not up to it. I shall do much better.

(Thunder rolls and Lupine laughs manically as the lights black out.)

SCENE 4 – CARROT'S ROOM

He is writing by candle light. After a moment, we hear his voice over the speakers, speaking his thoughts.

CARROT'S VOICE

Dearest father. Well, here I am in Ankh-Morpork. I don't think people here know right from wrong. I found Captain Vimes in a common ale-house. He told me to find a place to stay and report to Sergeant Colon at the Watch House tonight. He said, anyone wanting to join the guard needed their head examined. Perhaps that is done for reasons of hygiene.

I went for a walk. Then I saw some men trying to attack a young lady. I set about them. One of them tried to kick me in the Vitals, but I was wearing my protective and he broke his foot.

Then the lady came up to me and asked was I interested in Bed. I said yes. She took me where she lived. A boarding house, I think she said it was. It is run by a Mrs Palm. So I went upstairs and fell asleep . . . although it is a very noisy place, with people coming and going all the time.

The lady I saved – her name is Reet – came in and asked did I want anything, but they hadn't got any apples so I said no.

This afternoon I will go and look at the Thieves' Guild.

It is disgraceful what goes on here. If I do something about it, it will be a feather in my cap.

Your loving son, Carrot.

(The lights black out on Carrot and come up on the next scene)

SCENE 5 – THE PATRICIAN'S PALACE

The Patrician and Urdo Van Pew, President of the Thieves' Guild, are on stage.

PATRICIAN
He did what?

VAN PEW
Marched me through the streets. Me – Urdo Van Pew, President of the Thieves' Guild! In broad daylight! With my hands tied together!

You know very well that we have kept within the budget. To be humiliated like that! Like a common criminal!

(He starts to wag his finger at the Patrician. Klaxon. Action freezes. The Footnote enters)

FOOTNOTE
You need a special kind of mind to rule a city like Ankh-Morpork, and Lord Vetinari had it.

He appeared to have no vice whatsoever. Where other lords dined on larks' tongues, Lord Vetinari considered a glass of boiled water and half a slice of dry bread was an elegant sufficiency.

Under his hand, for the first time in a thousand years, Ankh-Morpork operated. It might not be fair or particularly democratic, but it worked. It was said he could tolerate absolutely anything except anything threatening the city.

(*she starts to exit*)

Oh. And mime artists. A strange aversion, but there you are. Anyone in baggy trousers and a white face who tried to ply their art in Ankh-Morpork would very quickly find themselves in the scorpion pit, on one wall of which was painted the advice: Learn The Words.

(*Klaxon. Action restarts. Footnote exits*)

VAN PEW
I have brought Captain Vimes here with me. There had better be a full apology, or you will have another strike on your hands.

(*The Patrician continues to gaze at Van Pew's finger with cold disdain. Van Pew becomes aware of the impropriety and withdraws the offending digit.*)

PATRICIAN
And you say this was one person?

VAN PEW
Yes! Er, that is . . .

PATRICIAN
But there are hundreds of you in the Guild building. Thick as, you should excuse the expression, thieves.

VAN PEW

Yes, but it was the way he just strode in as if he owned the place that fooled people. That and the fact he kept hitting people and telling them to mend their ways.

PATRICIAN

I shall deal with the matter momentarily.

VAN PEW

Does that mean 'now', or just 'briefly'?

(*The Patrician just looks at him*)

Er, a full apology, mark you. I have a position to maintain.

PATRICIAN

Thank you. Do not let me detain you.

VAN PEW

Right. Good. Thank you. Very well.

PATRICIAN (*pointedly*)

After all, you have such a lot of work to do.

VAN PEW

Well of course, this is the case. (*Hoping for a clue*) Er?

PATRICIAN

With so much business being conducted, that is.

VAN PEW

Er, I still don't quite follow.

PATRICIAN
Curious choice of targets (*referring to a piece of paper*) 'A crystal ball belonging to a fortune teller in Sheer Street, A small ornament from the Temple of Offler the Crocodile God.' And so on. Trinkets.

VAN PEW
I'm afraid I really don't know . . .

PATRICIAN
No unlicensed thieving, surely?

(*Klaxon. Action freezes. The Footnote enters*)

FOOTNOTE
Sorry to butt in again so soon. One of the Patrician's remarkable innovations was to form the city's thieves into a formal Guild and to make them responsible for theft. Thus, in return for an agreed level of crime per annum, and an undertaking to allow the City Watch to be wound down, the thieves saw to it that unauthorised crime was firmly stamped out. With crime levels agreed annually in advance, everyone could plan ahead, said Lord Vetinari, and part of the uncertainty had been removed from the chaos that is life.

The Watch hadn't liked it, but the fact was that the Thieves' Guild were far better at controlling crime than the Watch. After all, the Watch had to work twice as hard to cut crime by just a little, whereas all the Thieves' Guild had to do was to work less.

(*Klaxon. Action unfreezes as the Footnote exits*)

VAN PEW
Unlicensed thieving? Not while I remain President of the Thieves' Guild. We are most strict about that. I shall look into it directly. Depend upon it!

PATRICIAN
I'm sure I can. Thank you for coming to see me. Don't hesitate to leave.

(*As Van Pew exits, he meets Lupine Wonse entering*)

VAN PEW (*sotto voce to Wonse*)
It happens every time. You come here with a perfectly reasonable complaint. Next thing you know, you're shuffling out relieved to be simply getting away with your life!

LUPINE WONSE (*also sotto voce*)
You certainly have to hand it to the Patrician. If you don't, he sends men round to come and get it!

(*Van Pew exits. Lupine Wonse crosses to the Patrician.*)

PATRICIAN
The Watch appears to be having some difficulty with the Thieves' Guild. Van Pew was here claiming that a member of the Watch arrested him.

LUPINE WONSE
What for, sir?

PATRICIAN
Being a thief, apparently.

LUPINE WONSE
A member of the Watch?

PATRICIAN
I know. Vimes is outside, it seems. You and he were at school together, weren't you? Anyway, just sort it out, will you?

LUPINE WONSE
Yes, sir.

(*The Patrician exits through one door as Lupine Wonse goes to the other to summon Vimes.*)

Ah, Vimes. Did Mr Van Pew explain why he brought you here?

VIMES
No, sir. He seemed a bit . . . preoccupied.

LUPINE WONSE
Strange things afoot, Vimes. Serious complaint about you, I'm afraid.

VIMES
Sir?

LUPINE WONSE
Seems one of your Night Watch men arrested the head of the Thieves' Guild.

VIMES
Sorry, sir. Seem to have lost you there.

LUPINE WONSE

I said, Vimes, that one of your men arrested the head of the Thieves' Guild.

VIMES

One of my men?

LUPINE WONSE

Yes. Tied him up and left him in front of the Palace. Bit of a stink about it, I'm afraid. There was a note . . . signed by, erm, ah yes, Carrot Ironfoundersson.

VIMES

But we don't do that kind of thing. Arresting the Thieves' Guild? I mean, we'd be at it all day.

LUPINE WONSE

Apparently this Carrot thinks otherwise.

VIMES

Carrot? Name doesn't ring a bell.

LUPINE WONSE

He was quite . . . Carrot, Carrot, I've heard the name before. The volunteer, that was it! I showed you the letter from his father.

VIMES

The dwarf. Oh yes. You said we needed more ethnic minorities in the Watch.

LUPINE WONSE

Yes well. The Patrician wants an explanation. I don't

want to have to tell him that the Captain of the Night Watch hasn't the faintest idea what goes on among the men under his, and I use the term loosely, command. That sort of thing only leads to trouble, questions asked and so on. And we don't want that, do we?

VIMES
No, sir.

LUPINE WONSE
Of course we don't. So, because we went to school together I'll think of something to tell him and you, Captain, will make a point of finding out what's going on and putting a stop to it. Give this dwarf a short lesson on what it means to be a guard.

VIMES (*dutifully*)
Ha, ha, ha.

LUPINE WONSE
I'm sorry?

VIMES
Oh. Thought you made an ethnic joke there. Sir.

LUPINE WONSE
Look, Vimes, I'm being very understanding. In the circumstances. Now just get out there and sort it out.

VIMES (*saluting*)
Right you are, Mr Secretary, sir. I'll see to it that he learns that arresting thieves is against the law.

LUPINE WONSE
Very good.

(Lights out as scene ends)

SCENE 6 – A STREET IN ANKH-MORPORK

Night-time. Carrot and Cpl Nobbs are strolling along their beat.

CPL NOBBS
A cushy number, this route, Lance-Constable Carrot. You stick with me, I'll show you the ropes.

(*He tries a door handle*)

CARROT
Ah. I understand, Cpl Nobbs. We've got to see if anyone's left their store unlocked.

CPL NOBBS
You catch on fast, son.

CARROT
I hope I can apprehend a miscreant in the act.

CPL NOBBS (*uncertainly*)
Er, yeah.

CARROT
And if we find a door unlocked I suppose we must summon the owner. And one of us would have to stay to guard the premises, right?

CPL NOBBS
Yeah? I'll do that. No worry. And you could go and find the victim, er, owner.

CARROT
Back in the mountains, if a thief was caught, he was hung up by the—

CPL NOBBS
By the what?

CARROT
Can't remember. My mum used to say it was good for them, though. Oh, yeah, I remember now. It was by the town hall.

CPL NOBBS
What was?

CARROT
Where we used to hang them. Sometimes for days. They don't do it again I can tell you.

CPL NOBBS
'Ere, is it true you went into the Thieves' Guild and arrested the President?

CARROT
Yup.

CPL NOBBS
Bugger me.

CARROT

He seemed very cross about it, too.

CPL NOBBS

I can't think why! (*pause*) Why did you have to become a guard, lad?

CARROT

Everyone keeps asking me that. I didn't have to. I wanted to. My dad says it'll make a man of me.

CPL NOBBS

You mean you ain't running away from anything?

CARROT

What do you mean?

CPL NOBBS

Well, don't worry about it. So where're you stayin', lad?

CARROT

There's this lady called Mrs Palm—

CPL NOBBS

Rosie Palm's? Over in the Shades? What, every night? Bloody hell. And you've come here to have a man made of you? I don't think I'd like to live where you come from!

CARROT (*lost*)

Look, I came because my dad said it was the finest job in the world, upholding the law and everything. That's right, isn't it?

CPL NOBBS
Well, er, as to that . . . I mean, upholding the law . . . I mean ONCE, yes, before we had all these Guilds and stuff. The law sort of . . . um, it ain't really . . . everything's more . . . oh, I dunno. You keeps your head down and rings your bell.

(*shakes bell, not very vigorously, and calls, sotto voce*)

Twelve of the clock, and all's well.

CARROT
And that's it? No moonlight chases across the rooftops? No swinging on chandeliers?

CPL NOBBS
Chap could get hurt, that way. I'll just stick to the bell.

CARROT
Can I have a go?

(*Cpl Nobbs hands him the bell. He rings it very vigorously, and shouts.*)

TWELVE OF THE CLOCK AND ALL'S WELL!!!!!!

CPL NOBBS
Shhhh!

CARROT
Well, it is all well, isn't it?

CPL NOBBS
It won't be if you keep making that noise. Give it here!

CARROT

I don't understand. I've got this book . . .

(*he passes the* Laws and Ordinances *to Nobby*)

CPL NOBBS

Never heard of them. Now just stop all this, do you hear? Moonlight bloody chases, my bum!

CARROT

But, but, in this book it says . . .

CPL NOBBS

I don't want to know from no book.

CARROT

But it's the Law . . .

CPL NOBBS

Ah. Look. Here we are. An inn. The Mended Drum. And it's your shout, I think.

CARROT (*shouting*)

Alcohol Rots the Brain!

CPL NOBBS

No, no, when I said it's your shout, I didn't mean . . . never mind.

(*The Librarian passes across them and enters the Drum*)

CARROT

Wha— there's a monk . . .

44

CPL NOBBS

Don't say it! Don't say the 'm' word! It's the Librarian. Works up at the Wizards' University. Always comes down here for a drink of an evening.

(Klaxon. Footnote enters)

FOOTNOTE

Not many people these days remarked on the fact that he was an ape. The change had been brought about by a magical accident, and he was considered to have got off lightly. After all, he was still basically the same shape. He resisted all attempts to turn him back; he felt that life as an orang-utan had certain advantages over life as a human. It wasn't that he was unaware of the traumas of the human situation, it was just that, as far as he was concerned, you could stuff it.

(Klaxon. Footnote exits. Action unfreezes)

CARROT

But it's a mo—

CPL NOBBS

Don't! He's an orang-utan. An ape. Very particular about terminology. Can't stand being called a M-O-N-K-E-Y.

He used to be just like you and me. 'Cept he was a wizard. There was a magical explosion at the University a few years back. He got changed into an orang-utan.

CARROT

But, can't they change him back?

45

CPL NOBBS
Could do, I suppose. But he likes it the way he is.

CARROT
Oh. Hold on, what time is it?

CPL NOBBS
Well, it was midnight when you shouted it out a few minutes ago.

CARROT
And they're drinking in there?

CPL NOBBS
Yes?

CARROT
After hours? (*consults book*) in contravention of the Public Ale Houses (Opening) Act of 1678? Right!

(*He exits into the Drum. Short pause, then: there are off-stage crashes, shouts and bangs, as of a fight in progress. Vimes and Sgt Colon rush on*)

VIMES
Where is he? Where's the dwarf?

CPL NOBBS
What dwarf?

VIMES
Lance Constable Carrot, of course!

CPL NOBBS
He's a dwarf? I always said you couldn't trust them little buggers. Well, he certainly fooled me. He must have lied about his height. He's fighting, in there.

VIMES
All by himself?

CPL NOBBS
No, with everyone!

VIMES
I think we had better take prompt action.

(*They all jog, in formation, backwards into a nearby doorway*)

SGT COLON
S'right. A man could get hurt, standing over there.

(*After a while all goes silent. Carrot enters, looking slightly dishevelled. Vimes and Co. cross to him. He executes a salute, which Vimes acknowledges rather bemusedly*)

CARROT
Beg to report thirty-one offences of Making an Affray, sir, and fifty-six cases of Obstructing an Officer of the Watch in the Execution of his Duty, thirteen offences of Assault With a Deadly Weapon, six cases of Malicious Lingering, and . . . and Corporal Nobbs hasn't even shown me one rope yet.

(*He collapses to the floor as the lights black out*)

SCENE 7 – MEETING ROOM OF THE ELUCIDATED BRETHREN

All the Brethren and Wonse are on stage. Brother Watchtower is now wearing a humorous animal mask instead of his standard-issue Brethren mask.

LUPINE WONSE
Are the thuribles . . . WHAT are you wearing?

BROTHER WATCHTOWER
Er, sorry, Supreme Grand Master. I broke the other one and this was all they had down the shop.

LUPINE WONSE (*with a sigh*)
Right. Fine. Are the thuribles of Destiny ritually chastised, that Evil and Loose Thinking may be banished from this Sanctified Circle?

BROTHER DUNNYKIN
Yep.

LUPINE WONSE
Yep?

BROTHER DUNNYKIN
Yep. Done it myself.

LUPINE WONSE
You are SUPPOSED to say, 'Yea, O Supreme One'.

Honestly, I've told you often enough, if you're not going to enter into the spirit of the thing—

BROTHER WATCHTOWER
Yes, you just listen to what the Supreme Grand Master tells you.

BROTHER DUNNYKIN (*muttering*)
I spent hours chastising them thuribles . . .

BROTHER WATCHTOWER
Carry on, O Supreme Grand Master.

LUPINE WONSE
Very well then. Tonight we'll try another experimental summoning. I trust you have obtained suitable raw material, brothers?

BROTHER DUNNYKIN
. . . scrubbed and scrubbed, not that you get any thanks . . .

BROTHER WATCHTOWER
All sorted out, Supreme Grand Master.

LUPINE WONSE (*opening the bag*)
Ah, this is more like it.

BROTHER WATCHTOWER (*pointing to one item*)
I got that.

LUPINE WONSE
Yes, well done. Shows initiative.

49

BROTHER WATCHTOWER
Thank you, Supreme Grand Master.

BROTHER DUNNYKIN
. . . knuckles rubbed raw, all red and cracked. Never even got my three dollars back, either, no-one as much as says . . .

LUPINE WONSE (*speaking over Bro. Dunnykin*)
And now, we will commence to begin. Shut up, Brother Dunnykin.

   (*Lights out. Scene ends*)

SCENE 8 – A STREET IN ANKH-MORPORK

Sometime after Scene 6. Vimes, Cpl Nobbs, Sgt Colon and Carrot enter. All are much the worse for drink.

VIMES
Shame on, on, on . . . you. Drun' in fron' of a super, superererer ofisiler.

SGT COLON
Sss . . . sss . . . sssss . . .

VIMES
Put yoursel' onna charge. (*barges into a wall*) This wall assaulted me. Hah! You think you're tough, eh! Well, 'm an ofisler of the Law, I'llhaveyouknow, and we don' take any, any, any . . .

What's it we don' take any of, Sergeant?

SGT COLON
Chances, sir?

VIMES
No, no, no. S'other stuff. Never mind. Anyway we don' take any of, of it from anyone.

Shallie, shallie, shallie tell you something, Sarn't?

SGT COLON
Sir?

VIMES

This city. This city. T's'a woman. S'what it is. Ancient raddled old beauty. But . . . ifyoufallinlovewithher, then . . . she kicksyouintheteeth.

SGT COLON

City's a woman? (*Vimes nods*) But's eight miles wide, sir. 'S gotta river innit. Lots of houses and so on . . .

VIMES

Ah. Ah. Ah. Never, never, never said it was a SMALL woman, did I? Be fair.

We showed 'em, anyway. Well, Lance-Constable Carrot did. Hah! Taste of your own thingy, med'cine. Well, now you can bootle in your trems.

Two o'clock, and all's well!

CARROT

Where are we?

CPL NOBBS

On our way 'ome. Jus' goin' down . . . Sweetheart Lane.

SGT COLON (*the penny hasn't dropped yet – he corrects Nobby in the manner of one just discussing the best route from A to B*)

Nah, Sweetheart Lane's not on the way 'ome. It's in the middle of the Shades. You wouldn't catch us in the Shades after dark . . .

(*As one man, all but Carrot realise the horror of where they are*)

52

VIMES/COLON/NOBBS
THE SHADES!!!!

(*Klaxon. The Footnote enters. Action freezes*)

FOOTNOTE
Every town in the multiverse has a part that is something like the Shades. Ankh-Morpork's Shades were a sort of black hole of bred-in-the-brickwork lawlessness. Put it like this: even the criminals were afraid to walk the streets.

(*Footnote exits. Action restarts*)

(*They all cluster up to Carrot*)

SGT COLON
What're we goin' to do, Captain?

VIMES
Er, we could call for help . . .

CPL NOBBS
What? In the Shades?

VIMES
Yeh, p'raps not. Well that's one mistake we won't make again in a hurry . . . oh.

We must form a square.

(*They all try to form a point, behind Carrot. There is a noise of wings.*)

53

SGT COLON
　　Hey, what was that?

CPL NOBBS
　　What?

SGT COLON
　　There it is again. Sort of a leathery sound . . .

　　　　(*The sound continues*)

　　. . . or more sort of slithery . . .

　　　　(*There is a roar, and a flash of red light. Silence*)

　　　　(*Lights out*)

SCENE 9 – THE SAME STREET IN ANKH-MORPORK

The following morning. On stage are Vimes, Sgt Colon, Cpl Nobbs, Carrot, Lupine Wonse and the Patrician. Before them (4th wall) is the wall with the frieze of dead thieves.

PATRICIAN
  Hmm.

VIMES
  It seems to be the outline of three people, my Lord Patrician, in the brickwork. But the bricks all around the outline seem to have been subjected to an immense heat, which has vitrified the wall around it.

PATRICIAN
  Ye-e-s. And did your men do this?

VIMES
  Well, no sir.

PATRICIAN
  Good. I was going to say . . . vitrifying suspected criminals hardly constitutes use of minimum force, mm?

VIMES
  And did you see the footprints, my Lord Patrician? Well, footprints is stretching it a bit. They're more like talons.

PATRICIAN

I see. And do you have an opinion about all this, Captain?

VIMES

Well, sir . . . I know that dragons have been extinct for thousands of years, sir . . .

PATRICIAN

Yes?

VIMES

But, sir, the thing is . . . do THEY know?

PATRICIAN

So. You think an extinct, and indeed a possibly entirely mythical, dragon, flew into the city, landed in this narrow alley, incinerated a couple of criminals, and then flew away?

VIMES

Well, when you put it like that . . .

PATRICIAN

Don't you think someone would have noticed?

VIMES

Apart from them, you mean?

PATRICIAN

In my opinion, it's some kind of local warfare. Possibly a rival gang has hired a wizard.

VIMES

But there's the footprints, sir.

PATRICIAN

We're close to the river. Possibly it was a wading bird of some kind. But cover them up. We don't want anyone getting the wrong idea and jumping to silly conclusions, do we?

VIMES

As you wish, sir.

PATRICIAN

And paint over this.

VIMES

Is that wise, sir?

PATRICIAN

You don't think a frieze of ghastly shadows will cause comment?

VIMES

Not as much as the sight of fresh paint in the Shades, sir.

PATRICIAN (*irritated that he had not spotted this himself*)

Quite. True. Well, have it demolished, then. Carry on. Good show of initiative, that man. Patrolling in the Shades, too. Well done.

(*Carrot has stepped into his path. As he turns, he almost walks straight into Carrot*)

CARROT

Excuse me, sir. Is that your coach parked over there?

PATRICIAN
It is. Who are you, young man?

CARROT
Lance-Constable Carrot, sir!

PATRICIAN
Carrot. Carrot. Name rings a bell.

LUPINE WONSE
The young thief taker, sir.

PATRICIAN
Oh yes. A little error there, I think. But commendable.

CARROT
About your coach, sir. I couldn't help noticing that the front offside wheel, contrary to the . . .

SGT COLON
Lance-Constable Carrot! Attention! Lance-Constable Carrot, abou-uta turna! Lance-Constable Carrot, qui-uck marcha!

   (*and they exit*)

PATRICIAN
Carry on, Captain. And do come down heavily on any rumours about dragons, won't you?

VIMES
Yes, sir.

   (*The Patrician and Lupine Wonse exit*)

58

Look something is all wrong. The prints come out of the alley, but they don't go in. You don't get wading birds in the Ankh. The pollution'd eat their legs away.

So. Something big and fiery came out of this alley, but didn't come into it.

And the Patrician is worried about it.

(*Carrot and Sgt Colon enter*)

Any of you lot know anyone who might know anything about dragons?

SGT COLON
There's Lady Ramkin. Lives in Scoone Avenue. Breeds swamp dragons.

VIMES
Oh her. I think I've seen her around. The one with the 'Whinny If You Love Dragons' sticker on the back of her carriage?

SGT COLON
That's her. She's mental.

CARROT
What do you want me to do?

VIMES
Stay here. Keep prying eyes away until the workmen arrive to demolish that wall.

CARROT
You mean I'm in charge?

VIMES
In a manner of speaking. But you're not allowed to arrest anyone. Even if they're breaking the law. Understand?

CARROT
Yes. I'll read my book then.

(*Vimes, Sgt Colon and Cpl Nobbs exit. Carrot opens his book and starts to read. The Librarian enters and crosses to him*)

Ah, er, sorry. I'm supposed to stop anyone from looking at . . .

LIBRARIAN
Oook.

CARROT
Hello.

LIBRARIAN
Oook!

CARROT
Sorry?

LIBRARIAN (*with a heavy sigh*)
OOOK!

(*He beckons at Carrot to follow him*)

CARROT
I'm sorry. I can't leave here. I've had orders.

Someone hasn't committed a crime have they?

LIBRARIAN
Oook.

CARROT
A bad crime?

LIBRARIAN
Oook.

CARROT
Like murder?

LIBRARIAN
Eeek!

CARROT
Worse than murder?

LIBRARIAN
EEEK!

(*The Librarian grabs at Carrot's book and starts to run off*)

CARROT
Hey!

(*The Librarian brings back the book, and repeats the mime*)

Oh. Oh, I see. A book has been taken. From your Library?

(*The Librarian nods vigorously.*)

61

A BOOK has been taken? You're bothering the City Watch because a book has been taken? You think that's worse than murder?

This is practically a criminal offence, wasting Watch time. Why don't you just tell the head wizards at the University?

(*The Librarian does a brief mime*)

Oh, I see. They couldn't find their bums with both hands.

(*The Librarian nods.*)

Well, I don't see what I can do about it. What's the book called?

(*The Librarian scratches his head. Then, charade-style, he puts his palms together, and then folds them open*)

Yes, I know it's a book. What's its name?

(*The Librarian sighs heavily. He holds up four fingers*)

Oh. Four words? First word.

(*The Librarian holds two fingers close together.*)

Small word? A, The, Fo—

LIBRARIAN
Oook!

CARROT

The? The. Second word . . . third word? Small word. The? A? To? Of? Fro . . . Of? Of. The something of something. Second word. What? Oh, first syllable. Fingers? Touching your fingers? Thumbs?

(*The Librarian growls theatrically and tugs at its ear*)

Oh, sounds like. Er . . . Bum . . . Come . . . Dumb . . . Gum . . .

(*The lights fade down to indicate the passage of some time. 'Music While You Work' plays briefly. Lights up again.*)

. . . Numb . . . Plum . . . Rum . . . Sum . . . Sum. Sum! Second syllable. Small. Very small syllable. A. In. Un. On. On! Sum. On. Sum On. Summon! Summon-er? Summon-ing? Summoning. Summoning. The Summoning of Something. This is fun, isn't it! Fourth word. Whole word.

(*The Librarian attempts to mime the word 'dragons'*)

Big thing. Huge big thing. Flapping. Great big flapping, leaping thing. Teeth. Huffing. Blowing. Great big huge blowing flapping thing. Sucking fingers. Sucking fingers thing. Burnt. Hot. Great big hot blowing flapping thing . . . Politician?

(*The Librarian sighs very heavily*)

A great big hot blowing flapping thing. I give up. It could be anything. It could be a dragon, for all I know. Dragon! Dragons! That's it!

63

The Summoning of Dragons!

(*The Librarian raises its arms to heaven in thanks*)

This is serious! Come on, we've got to tell the Captain!

(*They exit as the lights black out*)

SCENE 10 – LADY RAMKIN'S HOUSE

Lady Ramkin is on stage. She is holding Errol. There are boxes behind her from which smoke rises gently. Vimes enters.

VIMES
Er, Lady Ramkin?

LADY RAMKIN
Ah. Hello. You don't know anything about matin', do yer?

VIMES
I, er, 'fraid not, my Lady. I'm Captain Vimes of the Night Watch. Ma'am.

LADY RAMKIN
Oh. Pity. Havin' a spot of trouble with this one. Goodboy Bindle Featherstone of Quirm. Can't cut the mustard ye'see. Wings're too small.

VIMES
Wings?

LADY RAMKIN
Yes. Dragons mate in the air dontcherknow. This poor chap just can't get airborne. One tries to breed for a good flame, depth of scale, correct colour and so on. One just has to put up with the occasional total whittle.

65

VIMES
Poor sod. Sorry, ma'am. Nice pets though.

LADY RAMKIN
Sound nice, grant yer. Then people realise it means soot burns in the shagpile, frizzled hair and crap all over yer furniture. Then they think it's getting too big and smelly and next thing it's either down to the Morpork Sunshine Sanctuary for Lost Dragons or the heave-ho into the river with a brick tied to yer neck, poor little buggers.

Now then. Captain Vimes was it?

Such a dashin' title, I've always felt. I mean, colonels are always so stuffy, majors are pompous, but one always feels somehow that there is something delightfully dangerous about a captain. What was it you wanted me for, Captain?

VIMES
Well, ma'am. I wondered. I was wondering, I mean, erm, how big swamp dragons grow?

LADY RAMKIN
I seem to recall that Gayheart Talonthrust of Ankh stood fourteen thumbs high, toe to matlock.

VIMES
Er . . .

LADY RAMKIN
About three foot six inches.

VIMES
No bigger than that?

LADY RAMKIN

Golly no. He was a bit of a freak, actually. Most don't grow much bigger than eight thumbs.

VIMES

Two feet?

LADY RAMKIN

Well done. That's cobbs of course. The hens would be smaller.

What's that you're carryin', Captain?

VIMES

Oh. Yes. This is a sketch I had made from some footprints we found in the Shades. There's a human footprint next to it to show the scale. Well, one of Corporal Nobbs's, anyway. Does it remind you of anything?

LADY RAMKIN

Large wadin' bird, p'raps?

VIMES

Oh.

LADY RAMKIN (*laughing*)

Or a really big dragon. Someone's been playin' tricks on you, old chap.

VIMES

Perhaps. But the prints were by a section of wall which had been vitrified by some great heat, and seemed to have completely carbonised three local citizens in the process. We were close by when it happened. Saw nothing except this very bright light. But we heard a sound like great leathery wings, and a great roar.

LADY RAMKIN (*hoarsely*)
Draco nobilis. The noble dragon. As opposed to these fellows, draco vulgaris the lot of 'em. But the big ones are all gone, yer know. Beautiful things. Weighed tons.

(*The sound of leathery wings has been increasing through-out her speech, and there have been noises of scuffling from the 'cages'. We hear noises of distant roaring, screams, and fire crackling. Flame effect*)

Biggest things ever to fly. No-one knows how they . . .

(*She points out into the fourth wall*)

My God! There it is! I would never have believed it if . . .

Do you realise we're seeing something which no-one has seen for centuries?

VIMES
Yes. Some bloody great lizard, setting fire to my city.

Of all the cities in all the world it could have flown into, it's flown into mine.

(*Carrot and the Librarian enter, followed by Cpl Nobbs and Sgt Colon*)

CARROT
Have you seen it? Have you seen it?

VIMES
We've all seen it.

CARROT
I know all about it. Someone's brought it here by magic.
Someone's stolen a book from the University Library.
It's called *The Summoning of Dragons*.

LIBRARIAN
Oook.

CARROT
It's about how to summon dragons. By magic.

LIBRARIAN
Oook.

CARROT
And that's illegal, that is! Releasing Feral Creatures
Upon the Streets, contrary to the Wild Animals
(Public—

VIMES
Oh Gods, this means wizards are involved. Is there
another copy of this book?

LIBRARIAN (*shaking its head*)
Oook.

VIMES
And you wouldn't happen to know what's in it? What?
Oh, four words. First word. Sounds like, bend, Bough?
Sow, Cow, How . . . How. Second word . . . small word,

To? to . . . yes, yes, understood, but I meant in any kind of detail. No. I see.

(*The noise has gone*)

CPL NOBBS
It'll be out there somewhere. Gone to ground, like, during the hours of daylight. It'll be sleeping on its dragon's hoard of gold and jewels.

VIMES
I expect you'd be interested in finding that hoard, wouldn't you, Nobby?

CPL NOBBS
Well, Cap'n, I was thinking about having a look around. You know, when I'm off duty, of course.

VIMES
You and most of the citizens of Ankh-Morpork, I should guess. This is going to be a bit of a growth industry, and someone is going to get hurt. Thanks for your help, milady. Come on, lads. We need to get to the main square. Pronto.

(*Lights out as they start to exit*)

SCENE 11 – THE MEETING PLACE OF THE ELUCIDATED BRETHREN

All on stage. Brother Watchtower is now wearing his, heavily repaired, 'real' mask

LUPINE WONSE
Once again, we have achieved success.

(*There is a ragged cheer, and the brethren dance around, some singing ''Ere we go . . .'*)

SILENCE!

You haven't done anything yet!

Do you imagine that real wizards prance around after every spell chanting ''Ere we go, 'ere we go, 'ere we go'?

BROTHER FINGERS
No, Supreme Grand Master.

LUPINE WONSE
Right.

BROTHER DUNNYKIN
There's no chance of us accidentally summoning it here, is there?

LUPINE WONSE

No, no. I assure you, Brother Dunnykin, that I, that is, we . . . have it under perfect control. The power is ours.

And now, there is the matter of the King.

BROTHER PLASTERER

Have we found him, then? That's a stroke of luck.

BROTHER WATCHTOWER

You never listen, do you? It was all explained last week. We don't go around finding him. We make a king.

BROTHER PLASTERER

I thought he was supposed to turn up. 'Cos of destiny.

BROTHER WATCHTOWER

Look, the Supreme Grand Master says we just find some handsome lad who's good at taking orders. He kills the dragon and Bob's your uncle. Simple.

BROTHER PLASTERER

But we could just get rid of the dragon ourselves. Stop summoning it. Everyone'll be happy.

BROTHER WATCHTOWER

Ho, yes. I can just see it? 'Hallo, we won't set fire to your houses any more, aren't we nice?' The whole point about a king is that he'll be—

LUPINE WONSE

An undeniably potent and romantic symbol of absolute authority.

BROTHER PLASTERER

Oh. Right. Stroke of luck then. Finding the true king right now.

LUPINE WONSE

For the last time, we haven't found the true king. We don't need the true king. I've just found us a lad who looks good in a crown, can take orders and can flourish a sword.

BROTHER WATCHTOWER

I suppose . . . he isn't the real heir to the throne?

LUPINE WONSE

What do you mean?

BROTHER WATCHTOWER

Well, you know how it is. Fate plays funny tricks. Haha. It'd be a laugh, wouldn't it, if this lad turned out to be the real king. After all this trouble—

LUPINE WONSE

THERE IS NO REAL KING ANY MORE!!!

What do you expect? Some people wandering in the wilderness for years patiently handing down a sword and a birthmark?

Some sort of MAGIC?

A few more nights of this and the people'll be desperate. They'd crown a one-legged troll if he got rid of the dragon. And we'll have a king. And he'll need an adviser, a trusted man, of course. Then there'll be no need for this dressing up. This ritual.

(Some mumbles of 'Ooooh' and 'I liked the dressing up' from the brothers)

Shut up! No more summoning the dragon.

I can give it up. I can give it up any time I like.

(Lights black out)

SCENE 12 – A STREET IN ANKH-MORPORK

On stage is Cut-Me-Own-Throat Dibbler, and a couple of warriors. They have just concluded their business with CMOT and are examining a poster. Vimes enters.

DIBBLER (*nodding in the direction of the warriors*)
Mornin' Captain. News spread quickly, eh?

VIMES
Morning Dibbler. What're you selling this time?

DIBBLER
Genuine article, Captain. Can't afford to be without it. Anti-dragon cream. Personal guarantee. If you're incinerated.

VIMES
What you're saying, if I understand you correctly, is that if I am baked alive by the dragon, you'll refund my money?

DIBBLER
Upon personal application. One dollar a jar, and I'm cutting me own throat. It's a public service, really.

VIMES (*reading the label*)
You've got to hand it to those ancient monks. Brewing it up so quickly.

So what's happening, Dibbler? Who're the guys with the swords?

DIBBLER
Dragon hunters, Captain. The Patrician's offering a reward of fifty thousand dollars to anyone who brings him the dragon's head. Not attached to the dragon. He's no fool.

VIMES
Fifty thousand dollars. I'm surprised you're not joining in.

DIBBLER
Ah well, I'm more what you might call the service sector. Here's my product list.

(*He gives Vimes a piece of paper*)

VIMES (*reading*)
Anti-dragon mirror shields, five hundred dollars . . .

Portable lair detectors, two hundred and fifty dollars . . .

Dragon-piercing arrows, one hundred dollars each . . .

Sacks, one dollar . . . Why sacks?

DIBBLER
On account of the dragon's hoard.

VIMES
Oh. Of course. And what are these?

(*He points to a length of stiff wire with a small piece of wood attached to the end*)

76

DIBBLER
Dragon detectors.

VIMES
How do they work?

DIBBLER
Well . . . you see this piece of wood at the end . . .

VIMES
Yes.

DIBBLER
Well, when that's burned through, you've found your dragon.

VIMES
Intriguing. Practical, whilst at the same time, almost completely useless. Well, good luck, Dibbler.

DIBBLER (*exiting*)
Thanks, Captain. I can do special rates for our boys in brown.

VIMES (*crossing to the warriors*)
What's all this?

FIRST WARRIOR
Cheap job. Fifty Thousand? Well below the going rate. Should be half his kingdom and his daughter's hand in marriage.

VIMES
But he's not a king, he's a Patrician.

FIRST WARRIOR
Well, half his patrimony then. What's his daughter like?

VIMES
He's not married. He hasn't got a daughter.

SECOND WARRIOR
No daughter? Wants people to kill dragons and he hasn't got a daughter?

VIMES
He's got a little dog he's very fond of.

FIRST WARRIOR
Bleeding disgusting, not having a daughter. And what's fifty thousand dollars these days, eh? You spend that much on nets.

SECOND WARRIOR
Right. Fifty thousand dollars? He can stuff it.

FIRST WARRIOR
Yeah. Cheapskate.

SECOND WARRIOR
Let's go and have a drink.

FIRST WARRIOR
Right.

(*They start to exit. Then they stop, and the First Warrior turns round*)

FIRST WARRIOR
What sort of dog?

VIMES
What?

FIRST WARRIOR
I said, what sort of dog?

VIMES
A small wire-haired terrier, I think.

(*The two warriors exchange glances*)

FIRST WARRIOR
Nah.

(*And they exit*)

VIMES
He's got an aunt in Pseudopolis, I believe.

(*The Librarian enters*)

LIBRARIAN
Oook?

VIMES
Oh. Hello. No, no luck yet, I'm afraid. I tell you what, you get back to the Library and see what you can find. I'll send word if we come up with anything.

(*At the Unicorn, we became aware now that the rest of the Watch were in the on-stage balcony, separately lit so that they appeared to be on the roof of one of the city's buildings. On a flat stage, this could be achieved with separately lighted areas, providing Vimes looks up when talking, as though addressing the men high up on a building, and the Watch look down when speaking to Vimes)*

You men seen anything yet?

(*The Librarian exits*)

And you can put that away for a start.

SGT COLON
But, sir—

VIMES
You know longbows are forbidden. Wait there.

(*He makes his way up to them*)

CARROT
That's right. The Projectile Weapons (Civic Safety) Act, 1634.

SGT COLON
Don't you keep on quoting all that sort of stuff. We don't have any of them laws any more! That's all old stuff! It's all wossname now. Pragmatic.

CARROT
Yes, but Captain Vimes says that he's not having his guards shooting citizens. We're here to protect and serve.

(Vimes enters)

Isn't that right, Captain?

VIMES
Er, yeah. Yes, that's right.

Anything?

CPL NOBBS
Nah. Bugger this for a game of soldiers. It's been scared off.

SGT COLON
Looks like it.

CARROT
And it's starting to get chilly. Maybe we ought to be getting down, sir? Lots of other people are.

VIMES *(who is staring fixedly at something)*
Hmm?

CARROT
Could be coming on to rain, too.

VIMES *(gently grabbing Colon's shoulder)*
Can you see anything odd about the top of that tower?

SGT COLON
Well, it looks like there's a dragon sitting on it, don't it?

VIMES
Yes, that's what I thought.

SGT COLON

Only, only, when you sort of look properly, you can see it's just made out of shadows and clumps of ivy and that. I mean, if you half-close one eye, it looks like two old women and a wheelbarrow.

(*They all try this*)

VIMES

Nope. It still looks like a dragon. A huge one. Sort of hunched up, and looking down. Look, you can see its wings folded up.

SGT COLON

Beg pardon, sir. That's just a broken turret giving that effect.

VIMES (*after a pause*)

Tell me, Sergeant – I ask in a spirit of pure enquiry – what do you think's causing the effect of a pair of huge wings unfolding?

SGT COLON

I think that it's caused by a huge pair of wings, sir.

VIMES

Spot on, Sergeant.

CPL NOBBS

Sodding arseholes!

VIMES

You are in uniform, Corporal Nobbs.

CPL NOBBS
Sorry, Captain. Sodding arseholes, sir.

VIMES
It shouldn't be that big. It's as long as a street . . .

(*Sound of leathery wings*)

CPL NOBBS
Look at it go!

CARROT
It's coming straight at us! Jump for it!

(*Carrot grabs the Captain and they all dive as we hear a roar and the light flares*)

(*Black out*)

SCENE 13 – CARROT'S ROOM

Carrot is on stage, writing one of his letters. We hear his thoughts over the speakers.

CARROT'S VOICE

Dear Father, Captain Vimes has been ill and is being looked after by a lady. Nobby says it is well known she is mental, but Sergeant Colon says it's just because of living in a big house with all them dragons, but that she's worth a fortune and well done to the Captain for getting his feet under the table.

I don't see what furniture's got to do with it.

Also I have made friends with this ape who's looking for his book. Nobby says it is a flea-bitten moron because it won eighteen pence off him in a game of Cripple Mr Onion, which is a game of chance with cards which I do not play. I have told Nobby about the Gambling (Regulation) Acts and he said Piss Off, which I think is in violation of the Decency Ordinances of 1389, but I have decided to use my discretion.

I will write again soon. Your loving son, Carrot.

(Lights out)

SCENE 14 – BEDROOM IN LADY RAMKIN'S HOUSE

Vimes is in bed. By his bedside is Cpl Nobbs.

VIMES
Uurrgh. Have I said 'Where am I?'

CPL NOBBS
No, sir.

VIMES
Where am I?

CPL NOBBS
Lady Ramkin's. She insisted we bring you here.

VIMES
Hang on. Hang on a minute. There was this huge dragon . . . headed straight for us . . . What happened?

CPL NOBBS
It was young Carrot. He grabbed you and the Sergeant and jumped off that roof just before the dragon got to us.

VIMES
My side hurts. He must have got me.

CPL NOBBS
No. I reckon that was when you hit the privy roof.

VIMES
What about Colon? Is he hurt?

CPL NOBBS
No, we're all all right. City's not looking too good, tho'. Dragon took out half the Wizards University, flamed a few other buildings, then it must of flown away.

VIMES
Anyone see where?

CPL NOBBS
Nah.

(*There is a knock at the door*)

LADY RAMKIN (*off stage*)
I say! Are you decent?

(*Cpl Nobbs crosses to the door.*)

CPL NOBBS
He's fine, ma'am. I was just going.

(*He exits*)

LADY RAMKIN
What a colourful little man Nobby is! A real character. We've been getting along famously. Amazing coincidence. My grandfather once had his grandfather whipped for malicious lingering, doncher know.

Now, about that dragon.

VIMES
What about it?

LADY RAMKIN
I've made some notes. It's a very odd beast. It shouldn't be able to get airborne. It should weigh about twenty tons. It's impossible!

VIMES
It dropped off that tower like a swallow . . . I knew there was something wrong. You've studied dragons? The big ones as well?

LADY RAMKIN
Oh yes. They're a great mystery, you know. There are legends, though. How one species started to get bigger and bigger and then . . . just vanished.

VIMES
Died out, you mean?

LADY RAMKIN
No . . . I think they just found somewhere where they could really BE.

VIMES
Really be what?

LADY RAMKIN
Dragons. Where they could really fulfill their potential. Some other dimension or something. Where the gravity isn't so strong, perhaps. We've got to find its lair.

VIMES
Yes.

LADY RAMKIN
But tomorrow will do. You need the rest.

VIMES
You're being very helpful. Look, erm, can I use your . . . er . . .

LADY RAMKIN
Yes, yes, of course. Through there. Can you manage?

VIMES (*with a hint of panic*)
Yes! Thank you!

(*He limps off*)

LADY RAMKIN (*sighing*)
What a charming man.

(*There is a loud knocking at the door*)

What on earth?

(*She crosses to the door. A small group of townspeople enter. They are carrying dragon detectors and makeshift weapons*)

Hwhat, is the meaning of this?

FIRST CITIZEN
Worl, it's the dragon, innit?

88

LADY RAMKIN
Hwhat about it?

FIRST CITIZEN
Worl. It's bin burning the city. They don't fly far. You got dragons here. Could be one of them, couldn't it?

SECOND CITIZEN
Yeah.

LADY RAMKIN (*grabbing a pitchfork*)
One step nearer, and you'll be sorry.

FIRST CITIZEN
Yeah? And what'll you do, eh?

LADY RAMKIN
I shall summon the Watch!

FIRST CITIZEN
Well, that's too bad. That's really worrying me, you know that? Makes me go all weak at the knees, that does.

SECOND CITIZEN
Yea. Stand aside, lady, because . . .

(*There is a flash – theatrical flash pod*)

VIMES (*entering with Errol*)
Hold it right there! This is Goodboy Bindle Featherstone of Quirm. The hottest swamp dragon in the City. It could burn your head clean off.

Now I know what you're all thinking. You're wondering, with all this excitement, has it got enough flame left

89

for another shot? And y'know, I ain't so sure meself. What you've got to ask yourselves is . . . am I feeling lucky?

FIRST CITIZEN
Now look, er, there's no call for anything like that.

VIMES
Drop it. Or you're history.

(*All but the First Citizen drop their weapons*)

Go ahead, punk, make my day.

(*First Citizen drops his weapon*)

But before you all disperse and go about your lawful business, just take a look at this dragon. Does he look sixty feet long? Would you say he's got an eighty foot wingspan?

SECOND CITIZEN
Who are you anyway?

VIMES
I'm Captain Vimes, City Watch.

VOICE IN THE CROWD
Night shift, is it?

VIMES (*realising he's in nightshirt and slippers*)
Right! Out with you! Go on!

90

FIRST CITIZEN
Right, right, we're going. No big dragons here, right enough. Sorry to have troubled you.

LADY RAMKIN
But before you go . . .

(*She produces a collecting box marked 'The Sunshine Sanctuary for Sick Dragons'. The crowd all put money in as they exit.*)

That was jolly brave of you.

(*Vimes is stroking the dragon.*)

I rather think he likes you.

VIMES
I thought you were going to get rid of him?

LADY RAMKIN
Well, yes, I suppose . . .

(*A pause. Then they speak together*)

LADY RAMKIN	VIMES
You don't think you might like . . .	How would it be if . . .

LADY RAMKIN
It'd be the least I could do. Please accept Goodboy as a gift, from a friend.

(*She crosses to Vimes and strokes the dragon as the Lights black out*)

SCENE 15 – CARROT'S ROOM

Carrot is on stage, writing a letter. Again we hear his voice over the speakers.

CARROT'S VOICE
Dear Father, Talk about a turn up for the books. Twice today groups of people have tried to search the cellars here for the dragon. It is amazing. And digging up people's privvies and poking into attics, it is like a Fever.

Sergeant Colon says when you're out on your Rounds and shout Twelve of the Clock and All's Well, while a dragon is melting the street, you feel a bit of a Burke.

This morning I went for a walk with Reet. She said I am different to anyone she's ever met. This afternoon we're going out with Captain Vimes and his new pet dragon to see if it can sniff out the other dragon. The Captain's dragon's got a really long name, but Nobby says it looks like his cousin Errol, so that's what we call it now.

I'll write again soon, Your loving son, Carrot.

   (*Lights out*)

SCENE 16 – A STREET IN ANKH-MORPORK

Vimes enters with Errol. Also with him are Lady Ramkin, Carrot and Sgt Colon.

SGT COLON
Dint work.

CARROT
Worth a try, though.

LADY RAMKIN
It could be all the rain, and people walking about, I suppose.

VIMES
We'd better get back.

(*Cpl Nobbs enters*)

CPL NOBBS
Some loony is going to fight it! Oh, sorry, begging your pardon, ma'am.

SGT COLON
I thought someone'd have a go. Poor bugger'll get baked in his own armour.

(*Noise of a trumpet*)

Look, there he is! Other side of the square! Smart sword, that. Go and see what's happening, Carrot.

(*Carrot exits. A few citizens enter and also look out of the fourth wall at the other side of the square. They are followed by Cut-Me-Own-Throat Dibbler*)

DIBBLER
Peanuts! Figgins! Sausages! Hallo, lads! Hello, Captain Vimes! Milady. In at the death, eh?

VIMES
What's going on, Dibbler?

DIBBLER
Some kid's ridden into the city and said he's goin' to kill the dragon.

(*Klaxon. Action freezes. Footnote enters*)

FOOTNOTE
The people of Ankh-Morpork had a straightforward, no-nonsense approach to entertainment. While they were looking forward to seeing a dragon slain, they'd be happy to settle instead for seeing someone being baked alive in his own armour. It would be something for the children to remember.

(*Klaxon. She exits. Action re-starts. A crowd starts to gather*)

DIBBLER
Got a magic sword, he says.

VIMES
Has he got a magic skin?

DIBBLER
You've got no romance in your soul, Captain. He says he's the rightful heir too. You know, heir to the throne.

VIMES
What throne?

DIBBLER
The throne of Ankh, of course. You know. Kings and that. Wish I could remember his name. I got an order in for two thousand coronation mugs. Gonna be a real bugger if I have to paint them all in by hand.

He made a big speech about how he was going to kill the dragon, overthrow the usurpers and right all wrongs. Everyone cheered. Sausage? Two for a dollar. Buy one for the lady? Made of genuine pig.

CARROT (*re-entering*)
Don't you mean pork?

DIBBLER
Manner of speaking. Certainly your actual pig products. No?

(*He moves over to the rest of the crowd, who, with Vimes and co., come gradually downstage to watch the 'king' (off in the fourth wall)*)

Get your pig sausages! Five for two dollars!

VIMES
It's all gone mad. What's going on, Carrot?

CARROT
There's this lad in the middle of the plaza. He's got a glittery sword. Doesn't seem to be doing much, though.

VIMES (*to Lady Ramkin*)
Kings. Of Ankh. And Thrones. Are there?

LADY RAMKIN
Oh yes. There used to be.

VIMES
Righting wrongs. What wrongs is he going to right? Eh?

FIRST CITIZEN
We-ell. There's taxes. They're wrong for a start.

SECOND CITIZEN
That's right. And the gutter of my house leaks something dreadful and the landlord won't do nothing. That's wrong.

FIRST CITIZEN
And premature baldness. That's wrong, too. Kings can cure that.

SECOND CITIZEN
They can't answer back, you know. That's how you can tell they're royal. Completely incapable of it. Has to do with being gracious.

FIRST CITIZEN
Money too. They don't carry it. That's how you can tell a king.

CPL NOBBS
Why? It's not that heavy.

FIRST CITIZEN
And. One of the main problems of being a king is the risk of your daughter getting a prick . . .

(*Vimes and co. hold their breaths, and glance at Lady Ramkin*)

. . . and falling asleep for a hundred years.

ALL
Aah!

CPL NOBBS
'Ere, we'd be in the ROYAL guard then. Plumes on our hats and all.

FIRST CITIZEN
Oh yes, pageantry. Very important that. Lots of spectacles.

SECOND CITIZEN
What, free?

FIRST CITIZEN
We-ell, I think maybe you have to pay for the frames.

VIMES
You're all bloody mad! You don't know anything about him, and he hasn't even won yet! It's a fire-breathing dragon! And he's just a guy on a horse, for goodness sake!

LADY RAMKIN
Dodgy buggers, kings. Some of them were fearful oiks. Wives all over the place, and choppin' people's heads off and so on. Not our sort of people at all.

(*Dragon noise. Flapping and roaring*)

VIMES
Oh, my god, this is it!

(*They all stare out front, horrorstruck. Noise of dragon landing. The 'king's' wimpy voice can be faintly heard: 'Now then, you vile and evil dragon, oh my word yes, take that!' The dragon roars, then the noise stops, suddenly, with a 'pop'.*)

(*A moment's pause, as the crowd take in what has happened, and then they all cheer*)

(*Black out*)

SCENE 17 – VIMES'S ROOM
Follows scene 16 with scarcely a pause.

Vimes is sitting on a chair. He is holding Errol and a piece of paper.

VIMES

I don't understand it, Errol. He hit it with the sword, and it just disappeared. Why didn't it fight? Why didn't it just burn him to charcoal? How can a sixty foot dragon be destroyed into utterly nothing?

Lady Ramkin says that when one of you little buggers explode, there's dragon everywhere. No offence. But there was no trace in the plaza. Not a trace.

And where did the king come from? Eh? I mean, he looked personable enough, I suppose. Good profile. Mind you, after killing the dragon, he could've been a cross-eyed dwarf for all that mattered.

Carried in triumph he was, to the Patrician's Palace. Patrician's been locked up in his own dungeons. Didn't seem to mind, though. He just smiled at everyone and went quietly.

It's too much of a coincidence, Errol.

Just when the city needs a king to rid it of a dragon, a king turns up.

Where did it come from? Where did it go?

Somebody called it, Errol. Somebody 'Summoned' it.
And somebody sent it away again.

(*He stands*)

But who?

(*Black out*)

SCENE 18 – DARK STAGE

We hear the voice of the Dragon over the speakers

DRAGON

Insolent fools! How dare they? How dare they? The power; the wind on my wings; the pleasure of the flame. And – what an interesting world: clear skies, and strange running creatures on the ground, to chase and incinerate.

And then! Then! Just as I was beginning to really enjoy it all, they cripple me – stop me from flaming – whip me back like some hairy canine animal.

They banished me, but there is still a path back. I can sense their leader's mind. The voice so full of its own diminutive importance; a mind almost like that of a dragon, but on a tiny scale.

I'll be back.

INTERVAL

SCENE 19 – A BAR IN ANKH-MORPORK

Cpl Nobbs, Sgt Colon, the Librarian and Carrot are on stage. The table in front of them is full of empty beer tankards. Carrot is still sober. Also on stage is the Footnote; she speaks first, while the scene behind remains frozen.

FOOTNOTE
Ankh-Morpork was celebrating. Street parties, knees-ups, pub crawls, posh banquets and balls. Lord Vetinari seldom had balls. In fact, there was a popular song about it. But now it would be balls all the way.

   (*Klaxon. She exits*)

SGT COLON
It's at times like this . . . threat to the city destroyed, reason to cebrelate . . . times like this, I wish old G . . .

CPL NOBBS
Don't say it. You agreed. We wouldn't say nothin'. No good talking about it.

SGT COLON
He was a righteous man, our Gaskin.

CPL NOBBS
We couldn't of helped it.

CARROT
What happened, then?

CPL NOBBS
He died . . . in the hexecution of his Duty.

LIBRARIAN
Oook!

SGT COLON
I told him. I said, Slow Down, You'll do yourself a chissmeef, erm, mischief. Dunno what got into him, running ahead like that.

CPL NOBBS
I blame the Thieves' Guild. Letting people like that on the streets . . .

SGT COLON
There was this bloke we saw done a robbery. Right in front of us! And Captain Vimes said Come On and we run. Only the point is, you shouldn't run too fast, see? Else you might catch them. Leads to all sorts of problems, catching people . . .

CPL NOBBS
They don't like it.

SGT COLON
They don't like it. But Gaskin went and forgot. He ran on, went round the corner and . . . well, this bloke had a couple of his mates waiting—

LIBRARIAN
Eeek!

CPL NOBBS
It was his heart really.

SGT COLON
Well anyway. And there he was. Captain Vimes was very upset about it.

You shouldn't run fast in the Watch, lad. You can be a fast guard, or you can be an old guard, but you can't be a fast old guard. Poor old Gaskin.

CARROT
It didn't ought to be like that.

LIBRARIAN
Oook!

SGT COLON
But it is.

CARROT
But it didn't ought to be.

LIBRARIAN
Oook!

SGT COLON
Well, it is.

(*Someone enters, carrying a box of bunting*)

CPL NOBBS
What's goin' on?

BUNTING CARRIER

Who wants to know, tiddler?

CARROT (*rising*)

We do, actually.

BUNTING CARRIER

Oh. Well, it's the coronation, innit? Got to get the streets ready; got to get the flags out. Reminders of our noble heritage.

CPL NOBBS

How long have we had a noble heritage, then?

BUNTING CARRIER

Since yesterday, of course.

(*And he exits with his box*)

CARROT

You can't have heritage in a day. It takes years.

SGT COLON

If we haven't got one, I'll bet we'll soon have had one. My wife left me a note about it. All these years, and she turns out to be a monarchist!

Huh! A man knocks his pipes out for thirty years to try and put a bit of meat on the table, and all she can talk about is some boy who gets to be king for five minutes' work. Know what I had for my tea last night? Bloody beef dripping sandwiches!

CPL NOBBS
  Cor!

CARROT
  Real beef dripping? The kind with the little crunchy bits on top? And shiny blobs of fat?

CPL NOBBS
  Can't remember when I last addressed the crust on a bowl of dripping. With just a bit of salt and pepper, you've got a meal fit for a k—

SGT COLON
  Don't say it!

CARROT
  The best bit is when you stick the knife in and crack the fat and all the browny gold stuff all bubbles up. A moment like that is worth a ki—

SGT COLON
  Shut up! Shut up! You're just—

CPL NOBBS
  You're just annoyed 'cos your wife's been embroidering crowns on her undies.

SGT COLON
  Not at all. But all this business about kings and lords. It's against basic human dignity. We're all born equal. It makes me sick.

CPL NOBBS
  Never heard you talk this way before, Frederick.

SGT COLON

That's Sergeant Colon, to you, Nobby.

CPL NOBBS

Sorry, Sergeant.

(*We hear the noise of the Dragon passing. They watch it pass them, as if it were just a passing cart*)

What the hell was that?

Here, you don't think . . .?

SGT COLON

We saw it killed, didn't we?

CARROT

We saw it VANISH.

SGT COLON

Nah. Probably just some . . . big wading bird. Or something.

CARROT

Maybe it is another dragon. We should warn people.

CPL NOBBS

Nope. Got a king now. Dragons is king's business. Up to him now.

(*Vimes carrying Errol, and Lady Ramkin enter hastily*)

VIMES

Come on, you men! Didn't you see it? It's back! We're tracking it with Errol!

(There is a roar. And the flash of light)

Oh, no! Not again!

(He rushes off)

LADY RAMKIN
Well, don't sit there like a lot of boobies! Come on!

(Lights down as they exit)

SCENE 20 – MEETING PLACE OF THE ELUCIDATED BRETHREN

All the brethren are on stage, except Lupine Wonse and Brother Fingers.

BROTHER WATCHTOWER
Are the Cups of Integrity well and truly suffused?

BROTHER DUNNYKIN
Aye, suffused full well.

BROTHER WATCHTOWER
The Waters of the World, are they Abjured?

BROTHER DOORKEEPER
Yeah, Abjured full mightily.

BROTHER WATCHTOWER
Have the Demons of Infinity been bound with many chains?

BROTHER PLASTERER
Damn. There's always something. It wasn't meant to be my job, but you sent Brother Fingers for the take-aways.

BROTHER WATCHTOWER
Just once, it would be nice to get the ancient and time-less rituals right, wouldn't it? You'd better get on with it.

BROTHER PLASTERER

Wouldn't it be quicker, Brother Watchtower, if I just did it twice next time?

BROTHER WATCHTOWER

All right. But you should call me Acting Supreme Grand Master, understand?

BROTHER DUNNYKIN

No-one said anything to us about you being Acting Supreme Grand Master.

BROTHER WATCHTOWER

Well, that's all you know because I bloody well am because Supreme Grand Master asked me to open the Lodge on account of him being delayed with all this coronation work. If that doesn't make me Acting Supreme Grand Bloody Master I don't know what does, all right?

BROTHER DOORKEEPER

I don't see why. You don't have to have a grand title like that. You could just be called something like, well . . . Rituals Monitor.

(*We hear the noise of the dragon approaching*)

BROTHER DUNNYKIN

Yeah. Don't see why you should give yourself airs. You ain't even been taught the ancient and mystic mysteries by monks, or nothing.

BROTHER DOORKEEPER
We've been hanging around for hours, too. I thought we'd get rewarded or something . . .

(*There is a bright flash and a roar. The stage lights black out, then up dim. We become aware that the black-robed figures now include Death. The brothers are not aware that the dragon has just flamed them*)

What the hell was that?

BROTHER WATCHTOWER
Lightning, I expect. Now look, lads, I expect the Supreme Grand Master will be along directly. Let's not spoil it now, eh, lads?

BROTHER DOORKEEPER
Okay.

BROTHER PLASTERER
Fair enough.

DEATH
CERTAINLY.

BROTHER DUNNYKIN
Yeah.

BROTHER WATCHTOWER
Er. Brothers? Brothers? We are all here, aren't we?

BROTHER DUNNYKIN
Of course we are.

BROTHER DOORKEEPER
Yes.

BROTHER PLASTERER
Why, what's the matter?

DEATH
YES.

BROTHER WATCHTOWER
Brothers? One, two, three . . . who's that? (*he sees Death. Short pause*) Is that you, Brother Doorkeeper?

DEATH
IN A MANNER OF SPEAKING.

(*Death puts his hand on Brother Watchtower's shoulder*)

BROTHER WATCHTOWER
Oooh, shit!

(*Black out. Death and the others exit, the Brothers leaving their robes on stage. As the lights come back up, Lupine Wonse enters, in his robe and mask. He stares, horrorstruck, at the 'bodies'*)

LUPINE WONSE
Oh my Gods

(*Voices are heard off stage*)

VIMES (*off*)
This way! Look, there! Come on!

SGT COLON (*off*)
Right, sir!

(*Wonse starts to sneak out. Vimes, Sgt Colon, Carrot, Cpl Nobbs and Lady Ramkin enter*)

VIMES
You! Stop!

(*Wonse runs off. Vimes starts to follow, but gives up and re-enters*)

LADY RAMKIN
Oh my goodness!

(*Brother Fingers enters, carrying the take-aways. He is horror-struck at the sight of his dead brethren*)

VIMES
Grab him!

(*Carrot does*)

Bring him over here. Excuse me, sir, but did you by any chance see—

BROTHER FINGERS
Mmmmuh! Mmmuh!

VIMES
What do you make of it, Sergeant?

113

SGT COLON
Looks like a sausage and pepperoni pizza with anchovies, sir.

VIMES
I meant the man.

BROTHER FINGERS
Nnnnnn.

SGT COLON
It looks like Benjy 'Fingers' Boggis to me, sir. Sly little bugger. Used to work over at the University. Odd-job man.

VIMES
Did he? So you'd have had access to the Library, eh?

BROTHER FINGERS
Whuuuh . . .

LADY RAMKIN
Can't we do anything for the poor man?

CPL NOBBS
I could kick him in the nuts for you if you like, m'lady.

BROTHER FINGERS
Dddrrr . . .

VIMES
Right. Take him to the Watch House. And no kicking him, even where it doesn't show. Understood?

CPL NOBBS

Yes, sir.

VIMES

Carrot, you stay with me.

(*Cpl Nobbs and Brother Fingers exit, followed by Sgt Colon and Lady Ramkin. Errol is fidgeting in Vimes's arms*)

VIMES

Look at him. He can't wait to get to grips with it. What good he thinks he'll do, God only knows. Game little devil, I'll give him that. Not nervous, are you lad?

CARROT

No, sir.

VIMES

No, you're not, are you? I suppose it's being brought up by dwarfs does it. You've no imagination.

CARROT

Thank you, sir. What do we do now, sir?

VIMES

Well, we'd better get along to the Patrician's . . . sorry, the King's Palace. Warn them about the dragon.

CARROT

I don't think they're going to be very happy.

(*They exit as the lights black out*)

SCENE 21 – THE PATRICIAN'S, sorry, KING'S PALACE. LUPINE WONSE'S OFFICE

Lupine Wonse is on stage. A servant enters.

SERVANT
There's a Captain Vimes to see you, sir.

LUPINE WONSE
Vimes of the City Watch?

SERVANT
Yes, sir.

LUPINE WONSE
Tell him to come back another day.

    (*Vimes and Carrot enter*)

VIMES
Good of you to see us.

LUPINE WONSE
Since you're here . . .

    (*Vimes chucks his helmet on Lupine Wonse's desk and sits down*)

. . . take a seat.

VIMES
Have you had breakfast yet?

LUPINE WONSE
Now really—

VIMES
Don't worry. Constable Carrot will see what's in the kitchens. Your servant can show him the way.

(*Carrot and the servant exit*)

LUPINE WONSE
There had better be a very good reason for . . .

VIMES
The dragon is back.

(*Pause*)

LUPINE WONSE
You've been drinking, haven't you?

VIMES
No. The dragon is BACK.

LUPINE WONSE
Now look—

VIMES
I saw it.

LUPINE WONSE
A dragon? You're sure?

VIMES (*shouting*)
No! I could be bloody mistaken! It may have been something else with sodding great big claws, huge leathery wings and hot, fiery breath! There must be masses of things like that!

LUPINE WONSE
But we all saw it killed!

VIMES
I don't know what WE saw! But I know what I saw!

Anyway, it's just flamed a house in Bitwash Street.

LUPINE WONSE
Any of them get out?

VIMES
Any of who?

LUPINE WONSE
The, er, people in the house. I assume there were people living there?

VIMES
It wasn't a normal house. It was the meeting hall for some secret society. Robes and so on.

LUPINE WONSE
A magic society?

VIMES
Could be. I saw another of 'em running away from the scene. Recognised his run from somewhere. I'll track him down.

LUPINE WONSE
No.

VIMES
No?

LUPINE WONSE
You're suffering from stress, Captain. Clearly this is just some magical society that's overstepped the mark and blown themselves up.

VIMES
What?

LUPINE WONSE
You're becoming obsessed about this dragon, Captain. Everyone saw it destroyed by our king.

VIMES
Yes, but—

LUPINE WONSE
No, Vimes. You've been injured and you've not given yourself the chance to properly recover. You're over-tired, and as such you're a liability. I'm going to have to insist that you take some leave of absence.

Give me your badge.

VIMES
My badge?

LUPINE WONSE
Yes. You're suspended until further notice.

(Vimes reluctantly hands over his badge)

Go home and rest, Captain.

(The Librarian enters)

VIMES
What is it?

LIBRARIAN
Oook.

VIMES
Errol? What's the matter with him?

LIBRARIAN
Oook!

VIMES
What's the right temperature for a dragon?

LIBRARIAN
Oook!

LUPINE WONSE
Look, fascinating although this is, would you mind discussing it elsewhere? Captain Vimes is supposed to be on leave.

LIBRARIAN
Oook?

VIMES
I'll explain later. Come on, let's see what's wrong with
Errol.

LUPINE WONSE
I don't want to see you at the Coronation tomorrow,
Vimes!

(*Black out*)

SCENE 22 – A TOWER OVERLOOKING THE PLAZA

On stage are Carrot, Sgt Colon and Cpl Nobbs. The noise of the procession can be heard.

CPL NOBBS
Doesn't seem right. The Captain should be down there, on the Plaza, for the coronation. It's his right. He's a Captain.

SGT COLON
Yes, but he's not, is he? Old Poncy Wonse made him hand in his badge, didn't he. Told you that. It's up to us. We got to do what he would've done. Guard the City. Watch for the dragon. I was looking forward to lining the streets. Bloody Day Watch got that job.

CPL NOBBS
I've never seen the Captain in such a filthy temper. I liked it better when he was on the drink. I reckon he's—

CARROT
You know, I reckon Errol is really ill.

SGT COLON
Yeah. Mebbe you're right, boy.

Still. We've got a good view from up here. If that dragon's alive, then it'll have got the hell away from here, I'm telling you. Not the right sort of place for dragons, a city. It'll have gone off somewhere where there's high places and plenty to eat, you mark my words.

CARROT
Somewhere like the city, you mean?

COLON/NOBBS
Shut up!

CPL NOBBS
Wind's getting up.

SGT COLON
Good. What was I saying?

CPL NOBBS
You were saying the dragon'll be miles away.

SGT COLON
Oh, right. Stands to reason, doesn't it? I mean, I wouldn't be hanging around here if I could fly away. If I could fly, I wouldn't be sitting on a roof on some manky statue, I'd—

CPL NOBBS
What statue?

SGT COLON
This one (*he gestures upwards with his thumb*). Up here. And don't try to give me the willies, Nobby, there's loads of old statues on the roof of this old dump.

CPL NOBBS

There's not, you know. They was all taken down last month when they re-leaded the roof.

(*They all turn and look upwards. Dragon noise. They turn and watch it fly out over the square*)

CARROT

Shouldn't we run and warn people? The King?

SGT COLON

Shouldn't bother. I think he'll soon find out.

(*We hear the king call to the dragon. 'Now then, you vile dragon, what is the—' There is a roar and a bright flash. Silence (or perhaps just a faint crackling noise, as of frying bacon?)*)

Nothing left. Just a wisp of smoke. Talk about king for a day.

CPL NOBBS

Got a new king now, by the look of it.

CARROT

The king is dead. Long live the dragon.

(*Black out*)

SCENE 23 – A ROOM IN THE PATRICIAN'S, yes all right, THE KING'S PALACE

A group of four local worthies, including the Chief Assassin and the Archchancellor of Unseen University, are on stage.

FIRST WORTHY
The way I see it, a dragon as king may not be a bad thing. When you think it through.

SECOND WORTHY
It definitely looked very gracious. Sort of, well, sleek. Nice and smart. Not scruffy. Takes a bit of pride in itself. The trouble with people today is they don't take pride in themselves.

CHIEF ASSASSIN
Well, speaking on behalf of the Guild of Assassins, we can see some benefits in the area of foreign policy.

FIRST WORTHY
How d'you mean?

CHIEF ASSASSIN
Diplomacy.

FIRST WORTHY
I don't know about that. I mean, your actual dragon, it's got these, basically, two sort of ways of negotiation, hasn't it? I mean it's either roasting you alive, or it isn't. Correct me if I'm wrong.

CHIEF ASSASSIN
    That's my point. Say the ambassador from Klatch comes along. You know what an arrogant bunch they are. Suppose he says, we want this, we want that, we want the other thing.

    Well, what we say is, shut your face unless you want to go home in a jar.

    (*Lupine Wonse enters. He looks a little crazed*)

LUPINE WONSE
    Ah, good, you're all here. Shall we all sit?

FIRST WORTHY
    Er . . . the note mentioned, lunch?

LUPINE WONSE
    Yes, later.

FIRST WORTHY
    With a dragon?

LUPINE WONSE
    Good grief, you didn't think it would eat you, did you? What an idea!

FIRST WORTHY
    Never crossed my mind. The very idea. Hahaha.

SECOND WORTHY
    Haha.

CHIEF ASSASSIN
Hoho. The very idea.

LUPINE WONSE
No, I expect you're all far too stringy. Haha.

ARCHCHANCELLOR
Haha.

CHIEF ASSASSIN
Ahaha.

LUPINE WONSE
I'm sorry things are a little . . . different, but the king hopes you will bear with it until matters can be more suitably organised.

SECOND WORTHY
The, er . . .

LUPINE WONSE (*his voice one dribble away from madness*)
The king.

(*He nods at the fourth wall. The Dragon is hanging from the ceiling of the hall in which they are meeting. All look up*) [*Perhaps your backstage people could provide some dragon breathing noises*]

SECOND WORTHY
Oh. The king. Right. Didn't see it there . . . er . . . Long life to him, I say.

LUPINE WONSE

The king graciously desires it to be known that it would be pleased to receive coronation gifts from the population at large. Nothing complex of course. Simply any precious gems or gold that they might have by them and can easily spare.

I should stress that this is in no way compulsory.

(The Chief Assassin resignedly starts to take off his rings. The two worthies also hand over their jewellery)

ARCHCHANCELLOR

Um . . . The king is no doubt aware that the Wizards' University has traditionally been exempt from taxes—

LUPINE WONSE

My dear sir . . . this is no tax. Any tribute would be entirely voluntary. I hope this is clear?

ARCHCHANCELLOR *(taking off rings)*

As crystal. And these contributions go—

LUPINE WONSE

On the hoard. The king recognises that there is little gold in Ankh-Morpork, but it intends to adopt a rigorous foreign policy to remedy this.

Privy Councillors . . . would of course be generously rewarded with lands and property seized.

CHIEF ASSASSIN

No doubt the, er, Privy Councillors would then respond with even greater generosity in the matter of, for example, treasure?

LUPINE WONSE
I am sure such considerations had not even crossed the king's mind. But the point is well made.

(*Wonse swallows hard, and continues*)

Which brings us on to a further matter of some delicacy, which I am sure well-travelled, broad-minded, ladies and gentlemen such as yourselves will have no difficulty in accepting.

I am referring . . . to the matter of . . . the king's . . . diet.

(*A silence*)

FIRST WORTHY (*in a hollow voice*)
Diet.

LUPINE WONSE
Yes.

ARCHCHANCELLOR
Er, we thought, that the dr—, the king, well, must have been arranging matters for himself, as it were.

LUPINE WONSE
Ah, but poor stuff, poor stuff. Stray animals and so forth. Obviously, as a king, such makeshifts are no longer acceptable.

SECOND WORTHY
Er, how often is the king hungry?

LUPINE WONSE
All the time. But it eats once a month. It's really more of
a ceremonial occasion.

FIRST WORTHY
And, er, when did the king last eat?

LUPINE WONSE
I'm sorry to say it hasn't eaten properly since it came
here.

FIRST WORTHY
Oh.

LUPINE WONSE
You must understand that merely waylaying people like
a common assassin—

CHIEF ASSASSIN
Excuse ME—

LUPINE WONSE
Some common murderer, I mean . . . there is no . . .
satisfaction there. The whole essence of the king's feeding is that it should be . . . an act of bonding between the
king and its subjects.

ARCHCHANCELLOR
The exact nature of this meal . . . are we talking about
young maidens here?

LUPINE WONSE
Sheer prejudice.

The age is immaterial. Marital status is, however, important. As is social standing.

It has to do with the flavour, I believe.

(He leans forward and whispers. His voice now pain-filled and urgent and, for the first time, genuinely his own)

Please consider it! After all, just once a month! The families of people of use to the king, Privy Councillors, for example, would of course be exempt.

And when you think of the alternatives.

(He leans back, speaking again for the dragon's benefit)

Well, gentlemen, perhaps we can consider all this over lunch.

CHIEF ASSASSIN
Er, perhaps not. Erm, urgent matters to deal with back at the Guild, you know. Some other time.

ARCHCHANCELLOR
Yes. Er, we'll let you have our decision soon.

LUPINE WONSE
Today.

ARCHCHANCELLOR
Today. Goodbye, Wonse.

CHIEF ASSASSIN
Goodbye.

(Wonse grabs the Chief Assassin's arm)

LUPINE WONSE (*through clenched teeth*)
Help. Me.

> (*The Assassin pulls his arm away and they start to exit.
> Wonse hisses after them*)

I can't run. It would find me. It would flame me.

> (*The Assassin has gone*)

DRAGON
No. Not you. I would not flame you.

> (*Wonse shrieks with surprise and falls to his knees before
> the Dragon*)

What does voluntary mean?

LUPINE WONSE
It means doing something of your own free will.

DRAGON
But they have no free will. They will increase my hoard,
or I will flame them!

LUPINE WONSE
But all the roaring and flaming. You don't need it.

DRAGON
Foolish ape! How else can I get them to do my bidding?

LUPINE WONSE
They'll do it of their own free will. And in time they'll

come to believe it was their own idea. It'll become a tradition. Believe me. We humans are adaptable creatures.

In fact, before long, if someone comes along and says a dragon king is a bad thing, they'll kill them themselves.

I know people, you see.

DRAGON
If you are lying—

LUPINE WONSE
No. You know I can't . . . not . . . to you.

DRAGON
And they really act like this?

LUPINE WONSE
Sorry. That's how we are. It's to do with survival I think.

DRAGON (*disappointed*)
There will be no mighty warriors sent to do battle with me?

LUPINE WONSE
I don't think so.

DRAGON
No heroes?

LUPINE WONSE
Not any more. They cost too much.

DRAGON
But I will be eating people!

And you have the effrontery to be squeamish. But WE are dragons, we are supposed to be cruel, heartless and terrible.

But I tell you one thing, ape. We never burned and tortured and ripped one another apart and called it morality.

LUPINE WONSE
Can I ask you a question?

DRAGON
Ask.

LUPINE WONSE
You don't NEED to eat people, surely? I think that's the only problem, from their point of view, you see.

DRAGON
NEED! Need! It is tradition that the finest flower of womanhood should be sent to the dragon to ensure peace and prosperity!

LUPINE WONSE
Yes, but you see, we have always been reasonably peaceful and prosperous—

(*The red lights come up and smoke jets onto the stage*)

DRAGON
DO YOU WANT THIS STATE OF AFFAIRS TO CONTINUE?

LUPINE WONSE
Of course.

DRAGON

Then the need is yours, not mine.

Now get out of my sight.

    (*Black out*)

SCENE 24 – LADY RAMKIN'S HOUSE

Lady Ramkin and Vimes are on stage. Errol is in/on a box upstage.

LADY RAMKIN
Damned if I know what's going on in there. What's he been eating?

VIMES
Last thing was a kettle.

LADY RAMKIN
Kettle of what?

VIMES
Nothing. Just a kettle. You know, handle, spout. Oh, and then we found him eating soot out of the chimney.

He whines a lot. I think he's trying to make a hot flame. I think he wants to challenge the big dragon. Every time it takes to the air he just sits there whining.

LADY RAMKIN
And doesn't explode?

VIMES
Not that we've noticed. I'm sure if he did we'd have spotted it.

LADY RAMKIN
And he eats indiscriminately?

VIMES
Hard to be sure. He sniffs everything, and eats most things. Two gallons of lamp oil, for example. We can't look after him properly. It's not as though we even need him to find the dragon now. I certainly bloody don't.

LADY RAMKIN
I think you're being very silly about this.

VIMES
Silly? I was sacked.

LADY RAMKIN
I'm sure it was all a misunderstanding.

VIMES
I didn't misunderstand it.

LADY RAMKIN
Well, I think it's because you're impotent.

VIMES
Wha—

LADY RAMKIN
Against the dragon, I mean. You can't do anything about it.

VIMES
I reckon this damned city and the dragon just about deserve one another.

LADY RAMKIN
> People are frightened. You can't expect much from them when they're frightened. Not everyone's as brave as you.

VIMES
> Me?

LADY RAMKIN
> With those people, when you stopped them taking my dragons.

VIMES
> Oh, that's not bravery, that's just people. People are easy.

LADY RAMKIN
> What will you do?

VIMES
> Don't know. I'm considering a number of options.

LADY RAMKIN
> I've got a lot of friends, you know. If you need any help, you've only got to say. The Duke of Sto Helit is looking for a new guard captain. I could put in a word for you. You'd like them. They're a nice young couple.

VIMES
> I'm not sure yet.

LADY RAMKIN
> I'm sure you know best.

VIMES
> Well then.

LADY RAMKIN
I expect you'll be wanting to be off, then.

VIMES
Yes, I expect I'd better be going.

LADY RAMKIN/VIMES
It's been very . . ./I'd just like to say . . .

VIMES
Sorry.

LADY RAMKIN
Sorry.

VIMES
No, you were speaking.

LADY RAMKIN
No, sorry, you were saying?

VIMES
Oh. I'll be off then.

LADY RAMKIN
Oh. Yes. Can't keep all these offers waiting.

(*They shake hands*)

VIMES
So I'll just be going, then.

LADY RAMKIN
Do call again. If ever you're in the area. I'm sure Errol would like to see you.

VIMES
Yes. Well, goodbye, then.

LADY RAMKIN
Goodbye, Captain Vimes.

(*He exits. She sighs, and crosses to Errol*)

Men!

(*There is a knock at the door. She crosses to it*)

Why, Captain Vimes, this is . . . who the hell are you?

(*She re-enters with two guards*)

Out with it. Don't just stand there. What do you want?

FIRST GUARD (*an incredulous tone in his voice*)
Lady Sybil Ramkin?

LADY RAMKIN
Use your eyes, young man. Who do you think I am?

FIRST GUARD
Well, I've got a summons for Lady Sybil Ramkin.

LADY RAMKIN
What do you mean, a summons?

FIRST GUARD
To attend upon the palace, like.

LADY RAMKIN
I can't imagine why it should be necessary at this time of the morning.

SECOND GUARD
If you don't come, we've been ordered to take steps.

LADY RAMKIN
If you think you'll lay a hand on me . . .

SECOND GUARD
No . . . but your pets might come to some harm.

FIRST GUARD
If they wasn't looked after properly, like.

LADY RAMKIN
You wouldn't!

I see. That's the way of it, is it? Two of you to fetch one feeble woman?

Very well.

(*She lashes out and punches the First Guard in the stomach. The Second Guard grabs her and holds her until the First Guard gets his breath back*)

FIRST GUARD
Bloody Hell! And the Dragon wants to eat HER?

SECOND GUARD
Yeah, well, she fits the bill. She's got to be the highest
born lady in the city. I don't know about maiden, but I
ain't asking!

(*Klaxon. Footnote enters, etc*)

FOOTNOTE
A number of religions in Ankh-Morpork still practised
human sacrifice, except that they didn't really need to
practise any more because they were so good at it. City
law said that only condemned criminals should be used,
but that was OK, because in most religions refusing to
volunteer for sacrifice was an offence punishable by
death.

(*Klaxon. She exits*)

SECOND GUARD
Come on.

FIRST GUARD
Weren't we supposed to kill her pet dragons?

SECOND GUARD
Nah, that was just a threat we was supposed to make.
The king's hardly likely to want us to go around killing
his kinsmen, is he?

FIRST GUARD
People do.

SECOND GUARD

Ah, that's different. That's 'cos WE'RE intelligent, innit.

(*Lights out as they exit*)

SCENE 25 – A ROOM IN THE PALACE

Night. Wonse enters, and starts searching around. After a moment, Vimes enters, carrying a book. He throws it to the floor in front of Wonse.

VIMES
Looking for this, were you?

LUPINE WONSE (*after a pause*)
OK. Clever of you to guess.

VIMES
Under the floorboards. Obvious, really.

LUPINE WONSE
I know. I suppose he didn't think anyone would be searching.

VIMES (*pleasantly*)
I'm sorry?

LUPINE WONSE
The Patrician. You know how he was for scheming and things. Obviously he called it up and then couldn't control it. Something even more cunning than he was.

VIMES
So what were you doing?

LUPINE WONSE

I wondered if it might be possible to reverse the spell. Or maybe call up another dragon. They'd fight then.

VIMES

A sort of balance of terror, you mean?

LUPINE WONSE

Could be worth a try. Look, about your job. We were both a bit overwrought at the time, so of course, if you want it back, there'd be no problem . . .

VIMES

It must have been terrible. Imagine what must have gone through his mind. He called it up, and then found it wasn't just some sort of tool but a real thing with a mind of its own. A mind just like his, but with the brakes off. You know, I wouldn't mind betting that at first he really thought that what he was doing was all for the best. He must have been insane. Sooner or later, I mean.

LUPINE WONSE

Yes, it must have been terrible. Ye gods, but I'd like to get my hands on him! All those years I've known the man, and—

VIMES

Run.

LUPINE WONSE

What?

VIMES

Run. I want to see you run.

145

LUPINE WONSE

I don't understan—

VIMES

I saw someone run away, the night that house in Bitwash Street was flamed. I remembered that run. When we were at school. It was you. 'Any of them get out', Wonse?

LUPINE WONSE

That's ridiculous. That's not proof.

VIMES

I know that. The way someone runs, the tone of voice . . . but what does it matter? Because even if I did have proof, there's no-one I could take it to, is there?

And you can't give me my job back.

LUPINE WONSE

I can! And you needn't just be a captain . . .

VIMES

You can't give me my job back, because it was never yours to take. I was never an officer of the city, or an officer of the king, or an officer of the Patrician. I was an officer of the law. It might have been corrupted and bent, but it was a law, of a sort. But now, there's no law except 'You'll get burned alive if you don't watch out.' Where's the place for me in there?

LUPINE WONSE

But you can help me! There may be a way to destroy the dragon, you see! Or at least mitigate the worst of it—

(Vimes punches Wonse, knocking him to the ground)

VIMES *(standing over him)*
The dragon's HERE! You can't channel it or persuade
it or negotiate with it. There's no truce with dragons.
You brought it here and we're stuck with it, you bastard!

LUPINE WONSE
What are you going to do?

*(Vimes doesn't answer. Wonse interprets this as a lack of
certainty)*

That's the trouble with you people. You're always
against anything attempted for the betterment of
mankind, but you never have any proper plans of your
own.

Guards! Guards!

Didn't expect that, did you? We still have guards here,
you know. Not many of course. Not many people want
to work here.

(Two guards enter)

VIMES
You'll never get away with it.

LUPINE WONSE
Oh, very original. But you're right. Then again, never is
a long time. None of us get away with anything for that
long.

You'll have time to reflect on this. Throw him in with
the Patrician.

FIRST GUARD
    Er—

    (*Klaxon. Action freezes. Footnote enters*)

FOOTNOTE
    Thick though the Palace Guards are, they are as aware
    as everyone else of the conventions of literature. When
    guards are summoned to deal with one man in over-
    heated circumstances it's not going to be a good time for
    them. The bugger's bound to be heroic. Lupine Wonse,
    on the other hand, doesn't read that kind of book.

    (*Klaxon. She exits. Action re-starts*)

LUPINE WONSE
    What's the matter, man?

FIRST GUARD
    You, er, want us to attack him?

LUPINE WONSE
    Of course, you idiot!

FIRST GUARD
    But there's only one of him.

SECOND GUARD
    And he's smilin'.

FIRST GUARD
    Prob'ly he's goin' to swing on the chandeliers, any
    minute. And kick over the table an' that.

LUPINE WONSE
He's not even armed!

FIRST GUARD
Worst kind that. They leap up, see, and grab one of the ornamental swords behind the shield over the fireplace.

SECOND GUARD
Yeah, and then they chucks a chair at you.

LUPINE WONSE
There's no fireplace, no chandelier, no sword! There's only him! Now take him!

(*They grab him tentatively*)

SECOND GUARD
You're not going to do anything heroic, are you?

VIMES
Wouldn't know where to start.

FIRST GUARD
Oh. Right.

(*Wonse exits. The two guards take Vimes over to the cell and put him in with the Patrician. Klaxon. Footnote enters*)

FOOTNOTE
Back again. It's a long walk down to the dungeons, and we don't to be bothered with that, do we? Vimes will shortly land in a pile of damp straw and in pitch blackness. We'll join him when his eyes have become

149

accustomed to the gloom and he realises he's in a dungeon which has not been designed for gracious living. At the far end a tiny grille lets in the merest suspicion of grubby, second-hand light. The bars are quite rusty, though. Vimes could probably work them loose eventually. Then all he'd have to do is to slim down enough to go through a nine-inch hole.

(*Klaxon. She exits. We are now in the dungeon. The Patrician is sitting at a table, reading a newspaper and drinking a glass of beer*)

PATRICIAN
Oh, Vimes, isn't it? I heard you were on the way down. Jolly good. Would you like a beer, Vimes?

VIMES
I see you're very comfortable here.

PATRICIAN
Never build a dungeon you wouldn't be happy to spend the night in yourself. The world would be a happier place if more people remembered that.

VIMES
We all thought you had built secret tunnels and such-like.

PATRICIAN
Can't imagine why. One would have to keep running. So inefficient. Whereas here I am at the hub of things. Never trust any ruler who puts his faith in tunnels and bunkers and escape routes. The chances are that his heart isn't in the job.

VIMES

Oh.

Do guards come in here?

PATRICIAN

Hardly ever. They don't bother about feeding me, of course. The idea is that one should moulder. In fact, up until recently, I used to go to the door occasionally and groan a bit every now and then, just to keep them happy.

VIMES

They're bound to come in and check, though?

PATRICIAN

Oh, I don't think I could tolerate that.

VIMES

How are you going to prevent them?

PATRICIAN

I thought you were an observant man. Did you look at the door?

VIMES

Of course I did. It's bloody massive.

PATRICIAN

Perhaps you should have another look.

You see, it's always the case, is it not, that should a city be overtaken by violent civil unrest, the current ruler is thrown into the dungeons? To a certain type of mind that is so much more satisfying than mere execution.

VIMES

Ye-es, but I don't see—

PATRICIAN

And you look at this cell door and what you see is a really strong cell door, yes?

VIMES

Of course. You've only got to look at the bolts and—

PATRICIAN

You know, I'm really rather pleased.

VIMES

Hold on. It's a perfectly normal dungeon door. It just depends upon your perspective.

All that's on the outside is the keyhole.

All the bolts and bars are on the inside!

PATRICIAN

Congratulations, Vimes. Knew you'd get there in the end. Now then, (*he refers to an article in the paper*) you might be interested to see this proclamation issued by the, er, king.

VIMES

'It has pleased . . . whereas . . . at the stroke of noon . . . a maiden pure, yet high-born . . . compact between the ruler and the city'

In my city! In my bloody city!

I'm not going to bloody well have it, understand?

PATRICIAN
I thought that might be your attitude.

VIMES
Now, my lord, just how do I get out of here?

(*A peanut flies in and lands on the table*)

What's this? A peanut?

PATRICIAN
Not mine, I assure you.

LIBRARIAN (*off stage*)
Oook.

VIMES
You! But how did you—?

(*There is a crash of masonry off stage. The Librarian enters, carrying the cell window and some of its surrounding masonry*)

Right! Let's get out of here! My Lord?

PATRICIAN
Er, no thank you, Vimes. I think I'm better off in here, pro tem. Ask your simian friend to replace the window on the way out, would you?

(*They exit. The Patrician smiles to himself as the Lights black out*)

SCENE 26 – A TOWER OVERLOOKING THE PLAZA

Cpl Nobbs and Carrot are on stage. [*We played this on a raised area, so that the impending 'Plaza' scenes could be played on stage level.*]

CPL NOBBS
I wonder who it'll be.

CARROT
What?

CPL NOBBS
The sacrifice, I mean.

CARROT
Sergeant said people wouldn't put up with it.

CPL NOBBS
Yeah, well, look at it this way: if you say to people, what's it to be, either your house is burnt down around you, or else some girl you've probably never met being eaten, well they might get a bit thoughtful. Human nature.

CARROT
What're we doing up here, then?

CPL NOBBS
Sgt Colon told me that we should meet him here. He's got a plan.

SGT COLON (*entering*)

Ah, lads, there you are. Right now, Nobby – you got your longbow?

CPL NOBBS

Yes, Sarge. Now, what's your plan?

SGT COLON

Good. When his majesty flies in to devour this maiden, you're goin' to shoot him in his voonerables.

CPL NOBBS

His what?

SGT COLON

His voonerables. I read it. All dragons have a voonerable spot.

You wait till it flies over and you say, Ooh look, there's his voonerable spot, and then you shoot 'im.

CPL NOBBS

It's a flippin' million-to-one shot, that is.

SGT COLON

Yes, BUT, when you really need them most, million-to-one chances ALWAYS crop up. Well-known fact.

CARROT

He's right, Nobby. You know that when there's just one chance which might just work – well, it works. I mean, it stands to reason. The gods wouldn't let it be any other way.

CPL NOBBS
I've fought of a problem.

CARROT
Wassat, Corp?

CPL NOBBS
What if it's not a million-to-one chance?

What if it's just a thousand-to-one chance?

(*Lights come up on stage level. The guards bring on Lady Ramkin. A small crowd follows, including the worthies, if possible*)

CARROT (*looking down*)
Oh, bloody hell!

SGT COLON
What is it?

CARROT
They've brought in the sacrifice. It's Lady Ramkin!

The buggers! Well-spoken lady like her, it's a disgrace!

SGT COLON
This is what it comes to, eh? Decent women can't walk the streets without being eaten! Right, you bastards, you're geography!

CPL NOBBS
History. It's history, not geography.

SGT COLON
Whatever. Give me the bow, Nobby.

(*Dragon noise*)

CPL NOBBS
Oh, shit.

SGT COLON
I'll bloody sort 'em.

CARROT
Sergeant!

SGT COLON
Look, just shut up, will you—

CARROT
Sergeant . . . it's coming!

CPL NOBBS
Run!

SGT COLON
There's no time!!

(*Flash of light and roar. The guards cry out. Black out
on tower. Lights up on square [stage level]*))

IN THE SQUARE

VIMES
You!

LADY RAMKIN
  You!

VIMES
  But why you . . .?

LADY RAMKIN
  Captain Vimes, you will oblige me by not waving that
  thing about and you will start putting it to its proper use.

  (*Dragon noise. Vimes cuts Lady Ramkin's bonds*)

FIRST GUARD
  What the hell do you think you're doing?

VIMES
  What the hell do you think YOU'RE doing?

SECOND GUARD
  It's coming back! Run!

  (*The crowd exit*)

VIMES
  Bastards. I wish . . .

  What's that noise?

  (*Dynamic music. Errol flies out above their heads*) [*Our
  Errol 'flew' out of a concealed box on stage, vertically into
  a masked area in the beams of our theatre. It would be
  even better if you could get yours to travel the full length
  of the auditorium, with smoke trailing from him!*]

LADY RAMKIN
It's Goodboy! Errol, I mean!

VIMES (*looking out into the fourth wall, again*)
Look at him go. He never looked as though he had it in him. Wrong shape, an' all that.

LADY RAMKIN
That's because we've only seen him on the ground. He's a natural flyer, but awkward on the ground – like seals in the sea, see?

VIMES
What's he doing? He can't stop that monster!

How do they fight? How do dragons fight?

(*Some of the crowd start to re-enter to watch. There is a noise of dragon fight*)

LADY RAMKIN
I, er . . . well, they just flap at each other and blow flame. Swamp dragons, that is.

(*Sgt Colon, Cpl Nobbs and Carrot enter*)

SGT COLON
Are you all right, ma'am? Did you see Errol go? What's he trying to do?

LADY RAMKIN
Protect US, I think.

CPL NOBBS
Come on, Errol! Add up the bastard!

SGT COLON
   Total, Nobby. Total the bastard.

CARROT
   There he goes, and . . . what's he doing with it? It looks
   like they're . . . playing?

VIMES
   Come on, Errol! Don't play around with it!

LADY RAMKIN
   It's difficult for Errol, he's so small, he's got no margin
   for error. He's got to hit it just right. IT only has to hit
   him.

VIMES
   Right. Wait! Where are they going? Why's Errol keep
   flying around it?

LADY RAMKIN
   This isn't right. They should be facing up to each other.
   Dragons only circle each other when . . . Oh.

   (*The music changes to something more romantic*)

VIMES
   What? When what? Oh.

CPL NOBBS
   Why don't you fight the bastard, Errol?

VIMES
   Bitch, Nobby. Not bastard. Bitch.

CPL NOBBS
Why don't you fi . . . what?

(*The dragon noises are now fading away*)

LADY RAMKIN
It's a girl.

CPL NOBBS
But it's soddin' enormous!

(*Vimes coughs, and looks at Lady Ramkin*)

A fine figure of a dragon, I mean.

SGT COLON
Er, wide, egg-bearing hips.

CPL NOBBS
Statueskew.

VIMES
Shut up. You men, come on with me. Quickly, while everyone's still watching those two.

CARROT
But what about the king? Or queen, or whatever?

VIMES
That's up to Errol. We've got other things to do.

CARROT
Where're we going?

VIMES
To the palace.

(*They exit as the lights black out*)

SCENE 27 – A ROOM IN THE PALACE

Wonse enters, looking furtive. He is clasping The Summoning of Dragons *and a sword. As he reaches a doorway, the Patrician steps out.*

PATRICIAN
Ah, Wonse.

LUPINE WONSE
Aah! You don't really exist. You're a ghost, or something.

PATRICIAN
I believe this is not the case.

LUPINE WONSE
You can't stop me! I've still got some magic left. I've got the book. I'll bring back another one! You'll see!

PATRICIAN
I urge you not to.

LUPINE WONSE
Oh, you think you're so clever, so in-control, so swave, just because I've got a sword and you haven't!

Well, I've got more than that. I've got the palace guards on my side. They never liked you. No-one likes you.

So it's back to the cells for you. And this time I'll make sure you stay there.

Guards! Guards!

(*Vimes and co enter*)

Take him away! Fetch more scorpions! Put him in the—

(*He realises it's Vimes*)

You!

PATRICIAN
Ah, Vimes, you will—

VIMES
Shut up.

Lance-Constable Carrot?

CARROT
Sir?

VIMES
Read the prisoner his rights.

CARROT
Yes, Sir.

Lupine Wonse, AKA Lupin Squiggle, pp Patrician . . .

LUPINE WONSE
What?

CARROT
. . . currently domiciled in the domicile known as the Palace, Ankh-Morpork. It is my duty to tell you that you have been arrested and will be charged with a number of

offences of murder by means of a blunt instrument, to wit a dragon, and many further charges of generalized abetting. You have the right to remain silent, you have the right not to be summarily thrown into a piranha tank. You have the right to trial by ordeal.

PATRICIAN (*calmly*)
This is madness.

VIMES
I thought I told you to shut up!

CPL NOBBS (*aside to Colon*)
Tell me, Sarge, do you think we'll like the scorpion pit?

CARROT
Erm, anything you say will be written down in my note-book and may be used in evidence.

PATRICIAN
Well, if this pantomime gives you any pleasure, Vimes. Take him down to the cells. I'll deal with him in the morning.

(*Wonse lunges at the Patrician, sword raised. Vimes steps in and parries the blade. Wonse drops the sword, and backs off*)

LUPINE WONSE
You'll be sorry. You'll all be very sorry!

VIMES
Oh, give it up, Wonse, for goodness' sake. Get him out

of my sight! Carrot, take him out onto the landing.
Throw the book at him.

(*Carrot and Lupine Wonse exit. A brief pause*) [*NOTE:
we couldn't do the 'book' bit on stage. If you can manage
the book throwing and Wonse's fall where the audience
can see it, so much the better. You can then amend the
preceding speech slightly, and omit the next couple of
lines*]

PATRICIAN
Er, Captain. I've noticed your man Carrot has a some-
what literal manner of thinking. Do you think that order
was wisely phrased?

VIMES
What do you . . .? Oh. Yes. Carrot!

(*There is a loud thump offstage and a groan followed by
a scream, cut off by a more sickening thump. Carrot
enters*)

CARROT
I'm sorry, Captain, he fell over the balustrade. It WAS
a very heavy book. It was an accident, sir, I—

VIMES
Don't worry lad—

PATRICIAN
Well, that will have saved the city some expense, I
suspect. Very well done. I suggest you give your men the
rest of the day off.

VIMES

Thank you, sir. OK lads. You heard his lordship.

PATRICIAN

But not you Captain. We must have a little talk.

(*The others exit*)

VIMES

Yes, sir?

PATRICIAN

Poor Wonse. I would have preferred him alive, you know.

VIMES

Sir?

PATRICIAN

Misguided, yes. But useful. His head could have been of further use to me.

VIMES

Yes, sir.

PATRICIAN

The rest we could have thrown away.

VIMES

Yes, sir.

PATRICIAN

That was a joke, Vimes.

You saved my life.

VIMES
  Sir?

PATRICIAN
  Let me give you some advice.

VIMES
  Sir?

PATRICIAN
  It may help you to make some sense of the world.

  I believe you find life such a problem because you think there are good people and bad people. You're wrong, of course. There are, always and only, the bad people – but some of them are on opposite sides.

  (*He walks downstage, and gestures out towards the audience*)

  A great rolling sea of evil. Shallower in some places, of course, but deeper, oh so much deeper in others.

  But people like you put together little rafts of rules and vaguely good intentions and say, this is the opposite. This will triumph in the end. Amazing!

  Down there, are people who will follow any dragon, worship any god, ignore any iniquity. All out of a kind of everyday, humdrum, badness.

  Not the really high, creative loathsomeness of the great sinners, but a sort of mass-produced darkness of the soul. They accept evil not because they say YES, but because they don't say NO.

I'm sorry if this offends you, Captain, but you fellows really need us.

VIMES (*quietly*)
Yes, sir?

PATRICIAN
Oh yes. We're the only ones who can make things work.

You see the only thing you good people are good at is overthrowing bad people. The trouble is it's the only thing you're good at.

One day it's ringing the bells and celebrating the overthrow of the tyrant. Next it's everyone sitting around complaining that no-one's taking out the trash.

Because the bad people know how to PLAN. Every evil tyrant has to rule the world. The good people just don't seem to have the knack.

VIMES
Maybe. But you're wrong about the rest! It's just that people are afraid, and alone . . .

They're just people. They're just doing what people do. Sir.

PATRICIAN
Of course, of course. You have to believe that, I appreciate. Otherwise you'd go quite mad. And now, there is such a lot to do. So you may go. Have a good night's sleep. Oh, and do bring your men in tomorrow. The city must show its gratitude. (*pause*) I said that you may go.

VIMES (*pausing at the door*)
Do you really believe all that, sir? About the endless evil and the sheer blackness?

PATRICIAN
It is the only logical conclusion.

VIMES
But you get out of bed every morning?

PATRICIAN
Hmm? Yes? What is your point?

VIMES
I'd like to know why, sir.

PATRICIAN
Oh, do go away, Vimes. There's a good fellow.

(*Lights black out. Lights up. Footnote enters with the Librarian*)

FOOTNOTE
What's this?

LIBRARIAN
Oook.

FOOTNOTE
Oh. THE book. Let's have a look. (*The Librarian passes it to her. She opens it and reads*) 'Yette draggons are notte lyke unicorns, I trow. They dwelleth in some Realme defined by the Fancie of the Wille, and Thus, it myte be that whomsoever calleth upon them, and giveth them

their pathway into thys Worlde, calleth forth theyre own Draggon of the Mind.'

So that's where they went. Into our imaginations.

What kind of man was Tubul de Malachite?

LIBRARIAN (*shrugging*)
Oook.

FOOTNOTE
Particularly evil?

(*The Librarian shrugs and shakes his head*)

If I were you, I'd put this book somewhere very safe. And Carrot's book of the Law, too. They're too dangerous.

LIBRARIAN
Oook.

FOOTNOTE
And now, let's go and have a drink.

LIBRARIAN
Oook.

FOOTNOTE
But just a small one.

LIBRARIAN
Oook.

FOOTNOTE
And you're paying.

LIBRARIAN
Eeek!

(*They start to exit*)

FOOTNOTE
Tell me, is it better . . . being an ape?

LIBRARIAN
Oook.

FOOTNOTE
Oh. Really? (*pause*) You know . . . this could be the start of a beautiful friendship.

(*And they exit. Lights out*)

SCENE 28 – THE PATRICIAN'S PALACE. NEXT DAY.

As many of the cast as possible are on stage. This includes Lady Ramkin. Vimes enters. There is some feeble applause and cheering.

LADY RAMKIN
Ah Captain. So good of you to come.

VIMES
Yes, well, Patrician's orders, wasn't it? I, er . . . look, erm, Errol—

LADY RAMKIN
What about him?

VIMES
Where do you think they've gone? Him and his . . . er, female.

LADY RAMKIN
Oh, somewhere isolated and rocky, I should imagine. Favourite territory for dragons.

VIMES
But it . . . SHE's a magic animal. What'll happen when the magic goes away?

LADY RAMKIN
Most people seem to manage.

Your men think you need looking after.

VIMES
Do they?

(*Sgt Colon, Cpl Nobbs, the Librarian and Carrot enter, smartly. More feeble cheering and applause from the crowd*)

SGT COLON
All present and correct, sah!

VIMES
Sergeant, just what have you been saying about me?

(*The Patrician enters. Feeble applause and cheering from the crowd. The Guard spring reasonably smartly to attention*)

PATRICIAN
Ah, yes. Stand easy, or whatever it is you chaps do. I'm sure we needn't stand on ceremony here. What do you say, Captain?

VIMES
Just as you like, sir.

PATRICIAN
Now, men, we have heard some remarkable accounts of your magnificent efforts in defence of the city.

Various public spirited citizens, including of course myself, feel that an appropriate reward is due.

VIMES
Reward?

PATRICIAN
It is customary for such heroic endeavour.

VIMES
Really haven't thought about it, sir. Can't speak for the men, of course.

SGT COLON
Permission to speak, sir.

(*The Patrician nods graciously. Sgt Colon coughs*)

[*Throughout the next lines, Vimes finds it increasingly hard not to laugh out loud at the ridiculousness of the situation*]

SGT COLON
Er, the thing is, saving your honour's presence, we think, you know, what with saving the city and every-thing, or sort of, or, what I mean is . . . we just had a go, you see, man on the spot and that sort of thing . . . the thing is we reckon we're entitled. If you catch my drift.

PATRICIAN
Do go on.

SGT COLON
So we like, put our heads together. A bit of a cheek, I know . . .

PATRICIAN
Please carry on, Sergeant. You needn't keep stopping. We are well aware of the magnitude of the matter.

SGT COLON
Right, sir. Well, sir. First, it's the wages.

PATRICIAN
The wages?

SGT COLON
Yes, sir. Thirty dollars a month. It's not right. We think
. . . we think a basic rate of, er, thirty-five dollars? A
month?

(*No reaction from the Patrician*)

With increments as per rank? We thought five dollars.

(*No reaction from the Patrician*)

We won't go below four. And that's flat. Sorry, your
Highness, but there it is.

(*Again, no reaction*)

Three, then?

PATRICIAN
That's it?

CPL NOBBS
There was another thing, your reverence.

PATRICIAN
Ah.

CPL NOBBS
There's the kettle. It wasn't much good anyway, and

then Errol et it. It was nearly two dollars. We could do with a new kettle. If it's all the same, your lordship.

PATRICIAN (*coldly*)
I want to be clear about this. Are we to believe that you are asking for a petty wage increase and a domestic utensil?

CARROT
Well, your honour, sometimes, we thought, you know, when we has our dinner break, or when it's quiet, like, at the end of the watch as it might be, and we want to relax a bit, you know—

PATRICIAN
Yes?

CARROT
I suppose a dartboard would be out of the question . . .?

(*In the silence we are aware of a barely restrained snorting. It is Vimes. Suddenly it all bursts forth in torrents of laughter, which continues until the lights fade out. The Patrician remains stony faced.*)

SGT COLON
I told you. I said the dartboard'd be pushing our luck. You've done it now.

(*Vimes laughs as the lights black out*)

SCENE 29 – OUTSIDE THE MENDED DRUM

Cpl Nobbs and Sgt Colon are on stage. Carrot enters, carrying three tankards of ale.

CARROT
Here we are, lads. Three pints. On the house.

SGT COLON
Bloody hell. I never thought you'd do it. What did you say to him?

CARROT
I just explained how it was the duty of all good citizens to help the guard at all times. And I thanked him for his co-operation.

CPL NOBBS
Yeah. And the rest.

CARROT
No, that was all I said.

SGT COLON
Ah well. Make the most of it, lads. While it lasts.

(*They all drink*)

What a time, eh?

CPL NOBBS
    If I never see any bloody king it'll be too soon.

CARROT
    I don't reckon he was the right king anyway.

    Talking of kings, anyone want a crisp?

SGT COLON
    There's no right kings.

    Ten dollars a month is going to make quite a difference.
    The notes my wife leaves me on the kitchen table are a
    lot more friendly now.

CARROT
    No. But I mean, there's nothing special about having an
    ancient sword. Or a birthmark. I mean . . . look at me.
    I've got a birthmark on my arm.

SGT COLON
    My brother's got one too. Shaped like a boat.

CARROT
    Mine's more like a crown thing.

CPL NOBBS
    Oho. That makes you a king, then. Stands to reason.

SGT COLON
    I don't see why. My brother's not an admiral.

CARROT
    And I've got this sword.

    (*He draws it. Chords, etc. Sgt Colon takes it*)

179

SGT COLON
It's a nice sword. Well balanced.

CARROT
But not for a king. Kings' swords are big and shiny and magical and have jewels, and when you hold them up they catch the light, ting.

SGT COLON
Yeah. I suppose they do.

CARROT
You can't go around giving people thrones 'cos of things like that. That's what Captain Vimes said.

CPL NOBBS
Nice job, mind. Good hours, kinging.

CARROT (*to himself*)
Unless. Maybe your real kings, in days of yore, you know, maybe they didn't have shiny swords, but just one that was bloody good at cutting things.

Just a thought.

CPL NOBBS
I say kinging's a good job. Short hours.

SGT COLON (*looking thoughtfully at Carrot*)
Yeah. Yeah. But not long days.

CPL NOBBS
Ah. There's that, of course.

CARROT
Anyway, my father says being a king's too much like hard work. It's not the kind of thing for the likes of us. Us – guards.

You all right, Sergeant?

SGT COLON
Hmmm? What? Oh, yes.

I'm sure it's all turned out for the best.

Best be off. What time is it?

CARROT
About twelve o'clock.

SGT COLON
Anything else?

CARROT
And all's well?

SGT COLON
Right. Just testing.

CPL NOBBS (*as they walk off*)
You know lad, the way you say it, I could almost believe it was true.

(*Lights fade out. Curtain calls*)

THE END

GUARDS! GUARDS! – PROPS LIST

On the furniture side, we just had a bed, plus a small table and some multi-purpose chairs (the inn, the Watch house, dungeon, etc). We re-used the door-with-a-hole-in that we'd built for the doorknocker in *Mort* by adding a sliding grille so it could be used for the Brethren's secret meeting-room. Also, we built some dragon pens: rough boxes – backs towards audience – from which smoke oozed gently, and a box that concealed the flying Errol.

Property	Scene Where First Used	Used By
Pickaxes	1	Dwarfs
Lanterns	1	Dwarfs
Spades	1	Dwarfs
Letter from Lupine Wonse	1	Carrot's Dad
Sword	1	Carrot's Dad
Copy: *Laws and Ordinances*	1	Carrot's Dad
'Protective'	1	Carrot's Dad
Copy: *The Summoning of Dragons*	2	Bro. Fingers
Notebook (containing secret knock)	2	Bro. Fingers
Klaxon on Pole	2	Footnote
Sword	2	Vimes
Masks	3	Brethren

Box or Bowl* for Magical Items	3	On stage
Magical Items (including amulet and some stones)	3	Brethren
Dagger	3	Zebbo Mooty
Scythe	3	DEATH
Same Box or Bowl*, now with ash	3	On Stage
Candle in Candlestick	4	On Stage
Writing Paper and Quill Pen	4	Carrot
List of Recent Thefts	5	Patrician
Report of Incident	5	Lupine Wonse
Halberd	6	Nobby
Bell	6	Nobby
Humorous Animal Mask	7	Bro. Watchtower
Bag of Magical Items	7	Bro. Watchtower
Errol	10	Lady Ramkin
Dragon Boxes	10	On Stage
Drawing of Dragon's Footprint	10	Vimes
Heavily Repaired Mask	11	Bro. Watchtower
Poster (Dragon)	12	On Stage

Tray of Goods (sausages, figgins)	12	Dibbler
Jar of Dragon Cream	12	Dibbler
List of Dragon Items	12	Dibbler
Sample Dragon Detector	12	Dibbler
Longbow	12	Colon
Dragon Detectors, Pitchforks	14	Crowd
Collecting Box	14	Lady Ramkin
Piece of Paper	17	Vimes
Tankards	19	The Watch
Box of Bunting	19	Man
Pizza Boxes	20	Bro. Fingers
Badge of Office	21	Vimes
Jewellery	23	City Worthies
Swords	25	Guards
Newspaper	25	Patrician
Glass of Beer	25	Patrician
Peanut (in shell)	25	Librarian
Cell Window + Masonry	25	Librarian
Flying Errol	26	On Stage
Sword	27	Lupine Wonse

TERRY PRATCHETT'S
MEN AT ARMS
The play
adapted by Stephen Briggs

'Alle Thee Dysk's a Stage'

Scarcely a year on from the events of *Guards! Guards!*, the Ankh-Morpork City Night Watch find their services are once more needed to tackle a threat to their city. A threat at least as deadly as a 60-foot dragon, but mechanical and heartless to boot. It kills without compunction. It is the first gun on the Discworld.

The original Watch – Captain Vimes, Sergeant Colon, Corporal Carrot and Corporal Nobbs – are joined by some new recruits, selected to reflect the city's ethnic make-up – Lance-Constables Cuddy (a dwarf), Detritus (a troll) and Angua (a w . . ., well, best to find out for yourself).

Stephen Briggs has been involved in amateur dramatics for over 25 years and he assures us that the play can be staged without needing the budget of Industrial Light and Magic. Not only that, but the cast should still be able to be in the pub well before closing time.

Oh, and a word of advice omitted from the play text:

LEARN THE WORDS   (Havelock, Lord Vetinari)

0 552 14432 0

THE DISCWORLD NOVELS OF TERRY PRATCHETT

THE FUNNIEST AND MOST UNORTHODOX FANTASIES IN THIS OR ANY OTHER GALAXY

MASKERADE

The show must go on, as murder, music and mayhem run riot in the night . . .

The Opera House, Ankh-Morpork . . . a huge, rambling building, where innocent young sopranos are lured to their destiny by a strangely-familiar evil mastermind in a hideously-deformed evening dress . . .

At least, he hopes so. But Granny Weatherwax, Discworld's most famous witch is in the audience. *And she doesn't hold with that sort of thing*.

So there's going to be *trouble* (but nevertheless a good evening's entertainment with murders you can really hum . . .)

'Pratchett is as funny as Wodehouse and as witty as Waugh'
Independent

Maskerade is the eighteenth novel in the now legendary *Discworld* series.

0 552 14236 0

TERRY PRATCHETT'S FAMOUS *DISCWORLD* SERIES
NOW AVAILABLE ON TAPE!

Seventeen titles in the now legendary *Discworld* series are now available in Corgi audio.

Also available in Corgi audio are six of Terry Pratchett's books for younger readers: *Truckers, Diggers, Wings, Only You Can Save Mankind, Johnny and the Dead* and *Johnny and the Bomb*.

'One of the best and one of the funniest English authors alive'
Independent

'Pure fantastic delight. If Terry Pratchett had put quill to parchment before Douglas Adams, Ford Prefect would still be stranded in the galaxy with his thumb in the air'
Time Out

Each title comes abridged on two tapes lasting approximately three hours.

0552 14017 1	THE COLOUR OF MAGIC	£8.99 incl VAT
0552 14018 X	THE LIGHT FANTASTIC	£7.99 incl VAT
0552 14016 3	EQUAL RITES	£8.99 incl VAT
0552 14015 5	MORT	£7.99 incl VAT
0552 14011 2	SOURCERY	£7.99 incl VAT
0552 14014 7	WYRD SISTERS	£7.99 incl VAT
0552 14013 9	PYRAMIDS	£7.99 incl VAT
0552 14012 0	GUARDS! GUARDS!	£7.99 incl VAT
0552 14010 4	MOVING PICTURES	£7.99 incl VAT
0552 14009 0	REAPER MAN	£7.99 incl VAT
0552 14415 0	WITCHES ABROAD	£8.99 incl VAT
0552 14416 9	SMALL GODS	£8.99 incl VAT
0552 14417 7	LORDS AND LADIES	£7.99 incl VAT
0552 14423 1	MEN AT ARMS	£7.99 incl VAT
0552 14424 X	SOUL MUSIC	£7.99 incl VAT
0552 14425 8	INTERESTING TIMES	£7.99 incl VAT
0552 14426 6	MASKERADE	£7.99 incl VAT
0552 14005 8	TRUCKERS	£7.99 incl VAT
0552 14006 6	DIGGERS	£8.99 incl VAT
0552 14007 4	WINGS	£8.99 incl VAT
0552 14008 2	ONLY YOU CAN SAVE MANKIND	£7.99 incl VAT
0552 14033 3	JOHNNY AND THE DEAD	£7.99 incl VAT
0552 14458 4	JOHNNY AND THE BOMB	£8.99 incl VAT

All Transworld titles are available by post from:

Book Service By Post, P.O. Box 29, Douglas, Isle of Man IM99 1BQ

Credit cards accepted. Please telephone 01624 675137, Fax 01624 670923
or Internet http://www. bookpost.co.uk for details.

Please allow for post and packing:UK: £0.75 per book Overseas: £1.00 per book

A LIST OF OTHER TERRY PRATCHETT
TITLES AVAILABLE FROM CORGI BOOKS

THE PRICES SHOWN BELOW WERE CORRECT AT THE TIME OF GOING TO PRESS. HOWEVER, TRANSWORLD PUBLISHERS RESERVE THE RIGHT TO SHOW NEW RETAIL PRICES ON COVERS WHICH MAY DIFFER FROM THOSE PREVIOUSLY ADVERTISED IN THE TEXT OR ELSEWHERE.

12475 3	**THE COLOUR OF MAGIC**	£4.99
12848 1	**THE LIGHT FANTASTIC**	£4.99
13105 9	**EQUAL RITES**	£4.99
13106 7	**MORT**	£4.99
13107 5	**SOURCERY**	£4.99
13460 0	**WYRD SISTERS**	£4.99
13461 9	**PYRAMIDS**	£5.99
13462 7	**GUARDS! GUARDS!**	£4.99
13463 5	**MOVING PICTURES**	£4.99
13464 3	**REAPER MAN**	£4.99
13465 1	**WITCHES ABROAD**	£4.99
13890 8	**SMALL GODS**	£4.99
13891 6	**LORDS AND LADIES**	£5.99
14028 7	**MEN AT ARMS**	£5.99
14029 5	**SOUL MUSIC**	£5.99
14235 2	**INTERESTING TIMES**	£4.99
14236 0	**MASKERADE**	£4.99
14237 9	**FEET OF CLAY**	£5.99
14161 5	**THE STREETS OF ANKH-MORPORK** (with Stephen Briggs)	£5.99
14324 3	**THE DISCWORLD MAPP (with Stephen Briggs)**	£5.99
14429 0	**MORT – THE PLAY (adapted by Stephen Briggs)**	£4.99
14430 4	**WYRD SISTERS – THE PLAY** (adapted by Stephen Briggs)	£4.99
14432 0	**MEN AT ARMS – THE PLAY** (adapted by Stephen Briggs)	£4.99
13945 9	**THE COLOUR OF MAGIC – GRAPHIC NOVEL**	£8.99
14159 3	**THE LIGHT FANTASTIC – GRAPHIC NOVEL**	£7.99
13325 6	**STRATA**	£4.99
13326 4	**THE DARK SIDE OF THE SUN**	£3.99
13703 0	**GOOD OMENS (with Neil Gaiman)**	£5.99
52595 2	**TRUCKERS**	£3.99
52586 3	**DIGGERS**	£3.99
52649 5	**WINGS**	£3.99
52752 1	**THE CARPET PEOPLE**	£3.99
13926 2	**ONLY YOU CAN SAVE MANKIND**	£3.99
52740 8	**JOHNNY AND THE DEAD**	£3.99
52968 0	**JOHNNY AND THE BOMB**	£3.99

All Transworld titles are available by post from:

Book Service By Post, P.O. Box 29, Douglas, Isle of Man IM99 1BQ

Credit cards accepted. Please telephone 01624 675137, fax 01624 670923, Internet http://www.bookpost.co.uk or e-mail: bookshop@enterprise.net for details.

Free postage and packing in the UK. Overseas customers: allow £1 per book (paperbacks) and £3 per book (hardbacks).